if she hid

(a kate wise mystery—book 4)

blake pierce

CHAPTER ONE

There are moments in every woman's life when they are expected to cry: weddings, giving birth, maybe during their children's first dance or marriage. But one moment Kate Wise had not expected to turn on the waterworks was watching her granddaughter crawl for the very first time.

She was babysitting for Melissa and Terry, as she had been doing once a week for the past month. They had made a commitment to make sure their marriage stayed fresh and exciting, pledging to have at least one date night a week. Kate kept little Michelle on those nights and, for the past five weeks, had been watching her granddaughter experiment with placing weight on her knees and forearms until, about five minutes ago, cooing and smiling, she had rocked back and forth in a push-up position.

"You're going to do it," Kate said, getting on the floor with Michelle. She could feel the tears even then, surprised by them but welcoming them at the same time.

Michelle looked at her, clearly pleased by the cheer in her grandmother's voice. She rocked forward then back...and then she crawled. She only made it forward by two motions before her arms went out from under her. But then she picked herself right back up and did it again.

"There you go," Kate said, clapping her hands. "Good girl!"

Michelle cooed at her again and then continued ambling forward on her clumsy little hands and feet.

Kate understood that it might not be the fact that Michelle was crawling that was making her cry. It was the look on the baby's face, the unadulterated trust and happiness in her little eyes when they found Kate's face. Michelle looked very much like Melissa had as a baby and the entirety of the situation was just too much.

They were sitting on a blanket on the floor, the blanket doubled over for added thickness in the event Michelle wobbled over. Other than the one time, though, she had not toppled at all. In fact, she was currently slapping at Kate's legs, as if demanding more attention. Kate picked her up, plopped her between her legs, and let Michelle grip her thumbs.

Kate simply enjoyed the moment. She'd watched her daughter grow up impossibly fast, so she knew how fleeting these moments

1

could be. She did feel a little guilty that Melissa and Terry were missing this milestone, though. She nearly called Melissa to let her know, but she didn't want to interrupt their date.

As she sat on the blanket playing with Michelle, someone knocked on her door. Kate had been expecting the knock, but Michelle jerked her little head in the direction of the door with an uncertain expression.

Kate wiped the last remnants of tears away from her face before saying, "Come on in."

The front door opened and Allen entered. He was carrying Chinese carry-out bags and, Kate was delighted to find, his overnight bag.

"How are my two favorite girls?" Allen asked.

"We're very mobile," Kate said with a smile. "This little stinker just crawled for the first time."

"No way!"

"Yes, she did."

Allen walked to the kitchen and took two plates out of the cupboard. As he divvied out their dinner onto the plates, Kate smiled. He knew his way around her house now. And he knew her well, too; for instance, he knew that she hated eating Chinese food out of those flimsy little containers and much preferred to eat it off of actual plates.

He brought dinner over to the living room, setting it on the coffee table. Michelle showed great interest in it and reached up. When she realized she could not reach it, she turned her attention to her toes.

"I saw you brought your overnight bag," Kate said.

"I did. Is that okay?"

"That's wonderful."

"I figured we could leave early in the morning and make that drive down to the Blue Ridge Mountains we keep talking about. Take in a few wine tours, maybe stay at a quaint little bed and breakfast in the mountains."

"That sounds nice. And spontaneous, too."

"Not too spontaneous," Allen chuckled. "We *have* been talking about it for about a month now."

Allen sat down across from her and opened his arms for Michelle to come over to him. She knew his face well enough and assumed the crawling position. She started over toward him, cooing all the way. Kate watched it all unfold, trying to remember a time when her heart had been this full.

She started to eat her dinner, watching Allen play with her granddaughter. Michelle was doing her little rocking-back-and-forth act while Allen cheered her on.

When Kate's phone rang, all three of them looked toward it. Even Michelle knew the sound of a cell phone ringer, her little hands reaching out for it as she moved into a seated position on the blanket. Kate plucked the phone from the coffee table, assuming it would be Melissa calling to check on Michelle.

But it wasn't Melissa. The name on the display read: Duran.

She was torn when she saw the name. A large part of her was excited at the prospect of helping out with a case. But the part that was enamored in the current moment didn't want to answer the phone. While it could be Duran simply calling with a question or research request—something he had been doing more and more these last few months—she also knew that it could be something more pressing and time consuming.

Kate could tell that Allen had already pieced together who was calling. Maybe he figured it out by the indecision on her face.

She answered the call dutifully, still quite proud that she was still actively working with the bureau despite being on the tail end of fifty-six.

"Hello, Director," she said. "To what do I owe the pleasure?"

"Good evening, Wise. Look…we've got a situation not too far from your neck of the woods. A double homicide and missing person. All the same case. It's got a small-town feel to it—so small that the local PD is admitting that they are unprepared for it. Because there's a missing persons element to it—the missing person being a fifteen-year-old girl—I'd like for you and DeMarco to try to wrap it quietly before the news hears about it and makes it a much harder case than it has to be."

"Any details yet?" Kate asked.

"Not many. But here's what I know so far."

As she listened to Director Duran, letting her know why he was calling and what he'd need her to do over the next twelve hours or so, she looked sadly at Allen and Michelle.

The call ended three minutes later. She set the phone back down and caught Allen looking at her. There was a tired smile of understanding on his face.

"So maybe we can try the winery and bed and breakfast thing some other weekend?" she said.

He smiled back sadly, then turned away.

"Yeah, maybe," he said.

He stared out the window, as if staring at their future, and Kate could see his uncertainty.

She couldn't blame him; she herself didn't know what her own future held.

But she knew one thing: someone was dead out there, and she damn sure was going to find out who did it.

CHAPTER TWO

While Kristen DeMarco was significantly younger than Kate (she had turned twenty-seven just a week ago), Kate had a hard time thinking of her as a young kid. Even when she was excited about starting on a new case, she managed to steep the excitement in the logic and gravity of the facts.

She was doing that now, as she and Kate headed west to the small town of Deton, Virginia. Kate had never been through Deton but had heard of it: a small rural town among a string of similar rural towns that dotted the northwestern edge of Virginia before West Virginia took over.

Apparently, DeMarco knew the town was nothing more than a small speck on the map as well. There was excitement in her voice as she went over the details of the case, but no real sense of urgency or expectation.

"Two nights ago, a Deton pastor visited the Fuller residence. He told police that he was there to collect several old Bibles from Wendy Fuller, the wife. When he arrived there, no one answered the door but he heard the television on inside. He tried the front door, found it unlocked, and shouted into the house to announce that he was there. According to the pastor, he saw blood on the carpet, still wet. He went inside to check things out and found both Wendy and Alvin Fuller dead. Their fifteen-year-old daughter, Mercy, was nowhere to be found."

DeMarco paused for a moment and then looked away from the file she had brought with her from DC. "Do you mind me doing this?" she asked.

"Going over the case? Not at all."

"I know it seems cheesy. But it helps me to retain the information."

"That's not cheesy," Kate said. "I used to carry a voice recorder on me at all times. I'd do exactly what you're doing right now and keep the recording on me at all times. So please...keep going. The details Duran gave me on the phone were scant at best."

"The coroner's report says the cause of death was multiple gunshot wounds, made with a Remington hunting rifle. Two shots to the father, one to the mother, who was also clubbed, probably with the butt of the gun. Local PD has checked hunting records and can confirm that the husband, Alvin Fuller, was a registered hunter

5

and owned that very same rifle. But it was nowhere to be found on the scene."

"So the murderer killed him with his own gun and then stole it?" Kate asked.

"Seems that way. Other than those notes, the local PD could come up with nothing, nor has the state PD found any real leads. Based on testimony from friends and family, the Fullers were considered to be good people. The pastor who discovered the bodies says they were at church almost every Sunday. He was collecting the Bibles from the Fullers to send overseas to missionaries in the Philippines."

"Good people don't always attract other good people, though," Kate pointed out.

"But in this kind of town…everyone knows everyone. It makes me think that if no one has offered any sort of evidence or theories, the killer might be an outsider."

"That's likely," Kate said. "But I think the fact that a fifteen-year-old girl is missing might be more important. Locals are of course going to assume that the girl was taken. But if we take that small-town filter away from it and don't assume that everyone is a good person, what others theories does that bring up?"

"That the daughter may not have been taken," DeMarco said. She spoke slowly, as if considering the idea very carefully. "That she may have run away. That she may be the killer."

"Exactly. And I've seen this sort of thing before. If we get into Deton spouting off that theory, we're going to get sour looks and closed doors."

"I assumed as much."

"That's not to say we don't treat it like a kidnapping case from the start. But we also can't go in assuming the daughter is the killer, either."

"Not until we know more about her," DeMarco said.

"That's right. And I feel like that's where we need to start. Because if everyone in town sees the Fullers as good people, I can pretty much promise you that no one is properly looking into the daughter as a suspect."

"So that's where we start," DeMarco said.

"Yes, but maybe under the radar. If they find out we're starting off with the fifteen-year-old daughter of the recently deceased as the primary suspect, this case is going to be much harder than it has to be."

It was a foreboding statement, one that seemed even more pressing as they passed by a sign that told them Deton was only seven miles ahead.

***

Deton wasn't quite as small as Kate had been expecting, but it was still quite rural. It seemed as if any business of any real importance was located along the main strip of highway that ran through the town. There was no Main Street, just a patch of Highway 44 that ran through it. Secondary roads meandered off of 44, snaking their way back into Deton's less populated area.

The bulk of the town consisted of a Rite Aid, a Burger King, a Dollar General, and several smaller local businesses. Kate had seen hundreds of little towns just like this during a career that had taken her all across the country and she felt that they all looked the same. Of course, that did not mean the people and their cultures were the same. To think such a thing would be a huge mistake.

The Fuller residence lay about three miles off of the main stretch of town, on one of the secondary roads. It was a simple two-story house in need of new siding and roofing. Its rustic look betrayed the other things that Kate and DeMarco noticed as Kate pulled into the driveway.

There was a news van parked in the driveway. A good-looking female reporter and a cameraman were talking something over by the front of the van. A single police car also sat in the driveway, an officer simply sitting inside. He saw Kate and DeMarco arrive and slowly started to get out of his car.

The reporter looked up as Kate and DeMarco got out of the car. Like some dedicated bloodhound, the reporter instantly came rushing over. The cameraman jostled his equipment, trying to follow behind, but fell a few steps short.

"Are you detectives?" the reporter asked.

"No comment," Kate barked.

"Do you have the authority to be here?"

"Do *you*?" Kate asked, biting back fast.

"I have a responsibility to report the news," the reporter said, giving a canned answer.

Kate knew the reporter would be able to find out the FBI had been called in within an hour or so. Therefore, she was fine with showing the reporter her badge as she and DeMarco walked toward the house.

"We're with the FBI," Kate said. "Keep that in mind if you get any ideas about following us inside."

The reporter stopped in her tracks, the cameraman nearly colliding with her. Behind them, the officer approached. Kate saw by the name tag and badge pinned to his uniform that this was the Deton sheriff. He grinned at the reporter as he passed them.

"See," he told the reporter rather gruffly. "It's not just me. No one wants you around."

He stepped in front of Kate and DeMarco, leading them to the front door. Under his breath, he added: "You know the laws as well as I do. I can't boot them because they're technically doing nothing wrong. Damned vultures are hoping a relative or someone will come by."

"How long have they been parked there?" DeMarco asked.

"There's been at least one news van parked there every day since this happened two days ago. At one point yesterday, there were three. This whole thing has made pretty big news around here. There have been news vans and crews located all around the county police station, too. It's pretty infuriating."

He unlocked the front door and ushered them in. "I'm Sheriff Randall Barnes, by the way. I have the displeasure of being the lead on this thing. The Staties found out the bureau was on the way and decided to step aside. They're still pursuing the manhunt for the daughter, but are leaving the murder part of the whole thing on my doorstep."

They stepped inside as Kate and DeMarco also introduced themselves. There was no conversation afterward, though. The sight before them, while not nearly as bad as some murder scenes Kate had seen, was jarring. The dried maroon splotches on the blue carpet were very much in-your-face. There was a stale feel to the place, something Kate had felt at scenes like this before—something she had tried describing countless times but always failed.

Out of nowhere, she thought of Michael. She had tried explaining the feeling to him once before, stating that it was almost as if a house itself could sense loss and that feeling of staleness in the air was the house's reaction. He had laughed at her and said it sounded almost spiritual in a weird way.

She was fine with that...mainly because it's exactly what she felt as she took a look around the Fuller home.

"Agents, I'm going to step back out onto the porch," he said. "Make sure we don't get any prying eyes. Holler if you need anything. But I'll tell you right now...anything you want to know

8

that's not already in the reports we sent over is going to have to come from one of my other officers—a fella named Foster. Here in Deton, we're not exactly used to cases like this. We're discovering just how unprepared we are for such things."

"We'd love to speak with him after this," DeMarco said.

"I'll give him a call and make sure he's at the station, then."

He left back through the front door quietly, leaving them to the scene. Kate stepped around the initial blood splatters on the carpet. There were some on the couch, too, and splatters on the wall just above the couch. A small coffee table sat in front of the couch and a few things on it seemed scattered—a few bills, an empty but overturned plastic cup, and the television remote. It could indicate signs of a quick struggle, but if so, it was not a particularly fierce one.

"No real signs of struggle," DeMarco said. "Unless their daughter is very strong and athletic, I don't see how she could have done this."

"If it *was* the daughter, they may not have seen it coming," Kate argued. "She could have come right into the room, hiding the gun behind her. One of them could have been dead before the other had any clue what was happening."

They studied the area for a few minutes, finding nothing out of the ordinary. There were a few pictures on the wall, several of which were family pictures. It was the first time she saw the girl she assumed was Mercy Fuller. The pictures showed her in varying stages of age: from around five to her current age. She was a cute girl who would likely become a beautiful girl sometime around college. She had black hair, brown eyes, and a radiant smile.

They then ventured deeper into the house, coming to a room that obviously belonged to a teenage girl. A bedazzled journal sat on a desk that was littered with pens and papers. A ceramic pink pineapple sat at the edge of the desk, a picture holder of sorts with a wire holder at the top. A picture of two teenaged girls, smiling widely for the camera, was held within it.

Kate opened up the journal. The last entry was from eight days ago and was about how a boy named Charlie had kissed her very quickly while they changed classes at school. She scanned a few of the entries before that and found similar scribblings: struggling with a test, wanting Charlie to pay more attention to her, wishing that bitch-face Kelsey Andrews would get hit by a train.

Nowhere within her room were there any indications of homicidal intent. They checked the parents' bedroom next and found it similarly disinteresting. There were a few adult magazines hidden away in the closet but other than that, the Fullers seemed to be squeaky clean.

When they exited the house after twenty minutes, Barnes was still on the porch. He was sitting in an old tattered lounge chair, smoking a cigarette.

"Find anything?" he asked.

"Nothing," DeMarco answered.

"Although I do wonder," Kate added. "Did you or the state police happen to find a laptop or cell phone in the daughter's room?"

"No. Now, on the laptop…that's not much of a surprise. Maybe you could tell by the state of the house, but the Fullers weren't exactly the type of family that could afford a laptop for their daughter. As for a phone, the Fullers' cell phone plan shows that Mercy Fuller did indeed have her own phone. But no one has been table to trace it just yet."

"Maybe it's powered down," DeMarco said.

"Probably," Barnes said. "But apparently—and this was news to me—even when a phone is off, it can be tracked back to the place where it was powered down…the last place it was on. And the state guys figured out it was last powered on here, at the house. But, as you pointed out, it's nowhere to be found."

"How many men do you have actively working the case?" Kate asked.

"Three at the station right now, just basically running interviews and digging through things like last purchases, last known places they visited and things like that. There's one guy left behind from the Staties that's helping, though he's not too happy about it."

"And you have one guy on your force that you'd consider the lead on it other than yourself?"

"Correct. As I said, that would be Officer Foster. The man has a mind like a lock box."

"Could you lead us to the station for a quick debrief meeting?" Kate asked. "But just yourself and this Officer Foster. Let's keep it small."

Barnes nodded grimly as he got up from the chair and flicked the last of his cigarette into the yard. "You want to talk about Mercy as a suspect without letting too many people know about it. Is that right?"

"I think it's foolish to rule it out as a possibility without looking into it," Kate said. "And while we look down that path, yes, you're right. The fewer people that know about it, the better."

"I'll make the call to Foster on our way to the station."

He walked down the steps, staring down the reporter and her cameraman. It made Kate wonder if he'd had at least one bad altercation with a news crew sometime during the last two days.

As she and DeMarco got into their car, she also gave the news crew a distrustful glance. She knew that in communities like Deton, a murder like this could be earth-shattering. And because of that, she knew that news crews in these areas would usually stop at nothing to get their story.

It made Kate wonder if maybe there was more of a story here than she was seeing—and if so, what she might need to do to get all of the pieces.

CHAPTER THREE

The Deton police station was about what Kate had expected. It was tucked away on the far end of the main stretch along the highway, a plain brick building with an American flag billowing at the top. A few patrol cars sat parked along the side of it, their meager numbers a reflection of the town itself.

Inside, a large bullpen area took up most of the space. A large desk sat at the front, unattended. Actually, the place looked basically deserted. They followed Barnes to the back of the building, down a thin hallway that boasted only five rooms, one of which was labeled by a placard on the door with *Sheriff Barnes*. Barnes led them to the last room on the hall, a very small room set up as a conference room of sorts. An officer sat at the table inside, rifling through a small stack of documents.

"Agents, meet Officer Foster," Barnes said.

Officer Foster was young man, probably creeping up on thirty years of age. He wore his hair in a buzzcut and had a scowl on his face. Kate could tell that he was a no-nonsense officer. He would not be cracking jokes to ease any tension and probably wouldn't bother with small talk to get to know the agents sitting in front of him.

Kate decided that she liked him right away.

"Officer Foster has basically served as the hub for this case ever since we got that call from Pastor Poulson," Barnes explained. "Any piece of information that has come through here has gone through his ears or eyes and he's added it to the case files. Any questions you have, he can probably answer."

"That's some lofty praise," Foster said, "but I can certainly do my best."

"Well, what do we have on information regarding who all three of the Fullers spoke with—aside from one another—before the murders occurred?" Kate asked.

"Alvin Fuller spoke with an old friend of his from high school as he was checking out at the Citgo out on Highway 44," Foster said. "He was coming home from work, stopped by to grab a six-pack of beer, and they ran into each other. The friend says they simply chatted about work and family. Very surface-level stuff just to seem polite. The friend said Alvin did not seem strange in any way.

"As for Wendy Fuller, the last person to speak to her other than her family was a co-worker. Wendy worked at the little shipping warehouse just outside of town. The co-worker in question said the last thing they spoke about was how Wendy was concerned that Mercy was starting to show a lot of interest in boys. Mercy had apparently had her first kiss recently and Wendy was afraid of what that could mean. But other than that, things seemed pretty much the same as always."

"And what about Mercy?" DeMarco asked.

"The last person she spoke with was her best friend, a local girl named Anne Pettus. We've spoken with Anne twice, just to make sure she told the same story. She said the last conversation they had was about a boy named Charlie. According to Anne, this Charlie kid was not Mercy's boyfriend. Anne also told us something that sort of bumps up against what her parents might have known about her."

"Like a lie?" Kate asked.

"Yes. According to Wendy's co-worker, they spoke about this supposed first kiss. But according to Anne Pettus, that's not true. Apparently, Mercy had her first kiss a very long time ago."

"Was she promiscuous?"

"Anne would not say as much. She just said that she knew for a fact that Mercy had done much more than kiss a boy."

"In regards to her disappearance, where does the evidence lean at this point?" Kate asked. "That she was taken or that she left of her own accord?"

"Unless the two of you found something new in the house, there is no evidence to suggest that Mercy was taken against her will. If anything, we have small pieces of circumstantial evidence that suggests she might have left on her own."

"What sort of evidence?"

"According to Anne, Mercy had a small amount of cash saved up. She even knew where she kept it: at the bottom of her sock drawer. We checked and there was about three hundred dollars hidden there. That actually goes against her leaving on her own because she would have taken that money, right? However, the last thing put on Mercy's credit card was a full tank of gas. She got it about two or three hours before her parents' bodies were found. Before that, two days prior, she purchased a few travel-sized cosmetics at a Target in Harrisonburg: toothbrush, toothpaste, deodorant. We have that in her credit card history as well as

13

confirmation from Anne Pettus, who went shopping with her that day."

"Did she happen to ask Mercy why she needed travel-sized cosmetics?" Kate asked.

"She did. Mercy said she was just low on stuff at home and hated to feel like a child asking her parents to buy her stuff."

"And no known boyfriend?" Kate asked.

"Not according to Anne. And she seemed to know just about everything about Mercy."

"I'd like to speak with Anne," Kate said. "Do you think she'd be open to it or are we going to get pushback?"

"She'd be very open to it," Foster said.

"He's right," Barnes added. "She's even called us a few times in between questioning to see if we have any new information. She's been very helpful. So have her folks, letting us talk to her. If you want, I can call and set something up."

"That would be fantastic," Kate said.

"She's a strong girl," Foster said. "But between you and me…I think she might be hiding something. Maybe nothing big. I think she just wants to make sure she doesn't convey anything bad about her missing best friend."

That's understandable, Kate thought.

But she also knew that the fact that they *were* best friends would be more than enough reason to hide something.

***

Anne's parents had understandably allowed her to stay home from school. When Kate and DeMarco arrived at the Pettus residence—located down a road very similar to the one the Fullers had lived on—the parents were standing at the front door, waiting. Kate could see them both through the glass screen door even as she parked the car in their U-shaped driveway.

Mr. and Mrs. Pettus stepped out onto their porch to meet the agents. The father kept his arms crossed, a sad look on his face. The mother looked tired, her eyes bloodshot and her posture worn down.

After a quick round of introductions, Mr. and Mrs. Pettus cut right to the chase. They were not rude or insisting, but simply concerned parents who did not intend to put their daughter through any unnecessary hell.

"She seems to get better each time she talks about it," Mrs. Pettus said. "I think as more time passes, she starts to understand that her best friend is not necessarily dead. I think the more the idea

14

that she might simply be missing sinks in, she wants to be of more help."

"That being said," Mr. Pettus added, "I would greatly appreciate it if you kept the questions brief and as hopeful as possible. Make no mistake…we won't interfere as you question her, but if we hear anything at all that seems to upset her, your time with our daughter is over."

"That's more than fair," Kate said. "And you have my word that we will tread carefully."

Mr. Pettus nodded and finally opened the front door for them. When they stepped inside, Kate saw Anne Pettus right away. She was sitting on the couch with her hands clasped between her knees. Like her mother, she looked tired and worn out. It then occurred to Kate that teenage girls tended to bond rather strongly with their best friends. She was unable to imagine the kind of emotions this young girl must be going through.

"Anne," Mrs. Pettus said. "These are the agents we told you were coming. Are you still okay with speaking to them?"

"Yes, Mom. I'm fine."

Both parents gave Kate and DeMarco a little nod as they sat down on either side of their daughter. Kate noticed that Anne didn't start to truly look uncomfortable until her parents flanked her.

"Anne," Kate said, "we will keep this quick. We've been filled in on everything you've already told the police, so we won't ask you to repeat all of those things again. Well, with one exception. I'd like to know about the shopping trip you and Mercy took out to Harrisonburg. Mercy purchased several travel-sized things, right?"

"Yeah. I thought it was weird. She just said she was running out of that stuff at home. Toothpaste, a small toothbrush, deodorant, things like that. I asked why she purchased them and not her parents but she sort of brushed it off."

"Do you feel she was happy at home?"

"Yeah. But I mean…she's fifteen. She loves her parents but hates it around here. She's been talking about moving away from Deton ever since we were ten years old."

"Any idea why?" DeMarco asked.

"It's boring," Anne said. She looked over at her parents apologetically. "I mean, I'm a just a bit older than Mercy; I'm sixteen and have a license and she and I go here and there sometimes. Shopping. The movies. But you have to drive like an hour to do any of that stuff. Deton is *dead.*"

"Do you know *where* she wanted to move?"

15

"Palm Springs," Anne said with a laugh. "She saw some show where people were partying in Palm Springs and thought it was pretty."

"Did she have any particular college she had her eye on?"

"I don't think so. I mean, at the little thing they had for us at school, she looked pretty hard at material from UVA and Wake Forest. But…yeah, I don't know."

"Can you tell us anything about Charlie?" Kate asked. "We saw her name in her journal and know they were at least familiar enough to share a quick kiss between classes. But the police told us that you said Mercy doesn't have a boyfriend."

"She doesn't."

Kate noticed right away how Anne's tone shifted a bit at this comment. Her posture seemed to go a little rigid as well. Apparently, this was a sensitive topic. But, being that she was only sixteen and her parents were both sitting beside her, Kate knew she could not directly accuse the girl of lying. She'd have to take another approach. Maybe there were some dark secrets concerning her friend that she simply did not want to voice.

"So are she and Charlie just friends?" Kate asked.

"Sort of. I mean, I think they maybe liked each other but just didn't want to date. You know?"

"Did she and Charlie ever do anything other than kiss that you know of?"

"If they did, Mercy never told me. And she tells me everything."

"Do you know if there were any secrets she was keeping from her parents?"

Again, Kate noticed an uneasiness settle across Anne's face. It was brief and barely there, but Kate recognized it from countless cases in the past—particularly where teenagers were involved. A quick dart of the eyes, shifting uncomfortably in their seat, either answering right away without thinking about their answer or taking far too much time to come up with an answer.

"Again, if she did, she never told me."

"What about a job?" Kate asked. "Was Mercy working anywhere?"

"Not recently. She was working like ten hours a week as a tutor for middle school kids a few months back. Algebra, I think. But they shut that down because there weren't enough kids interested in getting the help."

"Did she enjoy that?" DeMarco asked.

"I guess so."

16

"No horror stories from when she was tutoring?"

"None that she told me."

"But you feel confident that Mercy told you everything about her life, right?" DeMarco asked.

Anne looked slightly uncomfortable at the question. Kate wondered if it was perhaps the first time she'd been questioned in such a confrontational way—questioning something she had spoken as truth.

"I think so," Anne said. "We were...we *are* best friends. And I say *are* because she's still alive. I know it. Because if she's dead..."

The comment hung in the air for a moment. Kate could see that the emotion on Anne's face was real. Based on her expression, she could tell that girl would start crying soon. And if it came to that, Kate felt certain her parents would ask them to leave. It meant they likely didn't have much time—and that meant that Kate was going to have become a bit of a bully if she hoped to get some answers.

"Anne, we want to get to the bottom of this. And, like you, we are working under the assumption that Mercy is still alive. But, if I can be honest with you, with missing persons cases, time is the enemy. The more time that passes, the smaller our chances of finding her become. So please...if there is anything you might have been reluctant to tell the local Deton authorities, it's important that you tell *us*. I know in a town this small, you worry about what others will think and—"

"I think that's enough," Mr. Pettus said. He got to his feet and walked toward the door. "I don't appreciate you implying that our daughter has been hiding something. And you can look at her and tell that she's starting to get upset."

"Mr. Pettus," DeMarco said. "If Anne is—"

"We've been more than fair about letting her speak with the authorities, but we're done here. Now, please...leave."

Kate and DeMarco shared a defeated look as they got to their feet. Kate made about three steps for the door before she was stopped by Anne's voice.

"No...wait."

All four adults in the room turned toward Anne. There were tears rolling down her cheeks and a stern kind of understanding in her eyes. She looked at her parents for a moment and then quickly away, as if ashamed.

"What is it?" Mrs. Pettus asked her daughter.

"Mercy *does* have a boyfriend. Sort of. But it's not Charlie. It's this other guy...and she never told anyone because if her parents found out, they would have gone nuts."

"Who is it?" Kate asked.

"It's this guy that lives out near Deerfield. He's older...seventeen."

"And they were dating?" DeMarco asked.

"I don't think it was dating. They were sort of seeing each other. But when they got together, I think...well, I think it was just physical. Mercy liked it because there was this older guy giving her attention, you know?"

"And why would her parents not approve?" Kate asked.

"Well, the age thing for one. Mercy is fifteen and this guy is almost eighteen. But he's sort of bad news. He dropped out of high school, runs with a rough crowd."

"Do you know if the relationship was sexual?" Kate asked.

"She never told me. But I think it might have been because whenever I would joke with her and tease her about it, she'd get all quiet."

"Anne," Mr. Pettus said. "Why did you not tell the police?"

"Because I don't want people thinking bad of Mercy. She's...she's my best friend. She's kind and nice and...this guy is scum. I don't understand why she liked him."

"What's his name?" Kate asked.

"Jeremy Branch."

"You say he's a dropout. Do you know what he does for a job?"

"Nothing, I don't think. Tree work here and there, like cutting limbs and helping logging crews. But according to Mercy, he sort of just sits around his older brother's house and drinks most of the day. And I don't know for sure, but I think he sells drugs."

Kate almost felt sorry for Anne. The looks on the faces of her parents made it clear that she would be getting a stern talking to when Kate and DeMarco were gone. Knowing this, Kate walked over to Anne and sat in the place her father had been sitting only a minute before.

"I know this was hard for you," Kate said. "But you did the right thing. You've given us a lead and now maybe we can get to the bottom of things. Thank you, Anne."

With that, she gave a polite nod to Anne's parents and showed herself out. On the way to the car, DeMarco pulled out her phone. "You know where Deerfield is?" she asked.

"About twenty minutes deeper into the woods," Kate said. "If you thought Deton was small, you haven't seen anything yet."

"I'll call Sheriff Barnes and see if we can get an address."

18

She was doing exactly that as they got back into the car. Kate felt a sudden feeling of energy wash over her. They had a lead, the involvement of the local PD, and most of the day still ahead of them. As she pulled out of the Pettuses' driveway, she couldn't help but feel just a little hopeful.

CHAPTER FOUR

Although DeMarco had gotten a very clear address from Barnes, Kate couldn't help but wonder if Barnes had been wrong or if something had been lost in the transfer of communication. She saw the address five minutes after passing into the Deerfield town limits, plastered on the side of a dingy mailbox in black letters. But, like most everything else in Deerfield, Virginia, everything beyond the mailbox was open field and forest.

Roughly two feet from the mailbox, she saw the sketch-like lines of what she assumed was a driveway. Weeds had sprouted up along the side, hiding most of the entrance. She turned into the driveway and found herself on a narrow dirt road that led to a wider open space several yards ahead. She guessed she was looking into a large front yard that had simply not seen a mower in a very long time. There were three cars, two of which looked like total losses, parked in the yard. They were positioned along a dirt strip that served as the end of the driveway.

A few feet away from the cars, tucked not too far away from the tree line of the expansive forest beyond, was a doublewide trailer. It was the type that was decorated very much like a house from the outside and, if it had been properly cared for, would look like a rather nice place. But the front porch looked slightly slanted, one of the railings having fallen completely off. There was also a loose gutter on the right side of the house and, of course, the savagely overgrown yard.

Kate and DeMarco parked behind the junked cars and slowly made their way to the house. The grass, which was mainly weeds, came up to Kate's knees.

"I feel like I'm on some deranged safari," DeMarco said. "Got a machete?"

Kate only chuckled, her eyes on the front door. Stereotypes and Anne Pettus's information made her feel like she already knew what they would find inside: Jeremy Branch and his older brother, sitting around doing nothing. The place would probably smell like dust and mild garbage, maybe even like marijuana. There would be beer bottles scattered round cheap furniture, all of which would be pointed at a relatively nice television set. She'd seen the set-up countless times before, particularly when it came to young freeloaders living in rural areas.

They made their way up to the porch and Kate knocked on the door. She could hear the murmur of music coming from inside, something heavy but at a low volume. She also heard heavy footsteps approaching the door. When it opened several seconds later, she was greeted by a young-looking man dressed in a tank top and a pair of khaki shorts. A five o'clock shadow bordered his face. His entire left arm was covered in tattoos and both ears were pierced.

He smiled at the sight of the two women on his porch at first but then the reality of the situation seemed to catch up with him. It wasn't just two women—it was two women dressed in a professional manner with serious looks on their faces.

"Who are you?" he asked.

DeMarco showed her badge, taking a step closer to the door. "Agents DeMarco and Wise," she said. "We were hoping to get a word with Jeremy Branch."

The young man looked legitimately confused and slightly scared. He took a small step back away from the door, looking back and forth between them with caution. "That's…well, that's me. But what do you need me for?"

"We assume you've heard the news about a girl over in Deton by now," Kate said. "A girl by the name of Mercy Fuller."

The look on his face told Kate all she needed to know. Without saying a word, Jeremy all but confirmed that he knew Mercy. He nodded and then looked back into the trailer, maybe for assistance from his older brother.

"Can you confirm that for me?" Kate asked.

"Yeah, I heard. She went missing. Her parents were killed, right?"

"Right. Mr. Branch, can we please come in and talk for a moment?"

"Well, it's not my place. It belongs to my brother. And I don't know if he…"

"I don't know if you know how this works or not," Kate said. "We'd like to come in and chat. We can do it here or, based on what we've heard about you, we can do it at the police station over in Deton. It's your choice."

"Oh," he said. The kid looked absolutely cornered, like a threatened animal looking for a way out. "Well, then, I guess I can—"

He then interrupted himself by slamming the door in their faces. After the thunderous slam and a quick jerk back from the unexpected action, Kate could hear quick footfalls in the house.

"He's on the run," Kate said.

But before she could open the door again, DeMarco was already leaping down from the porch and heading to the back of the trailer. Kate drew her sidearm, pushed the door open, and stepped inside.

She heard just a few more footsteps from further in the trailer and then the sound of another door opening. *A back door,* Kate thought. *Hopefully DeMarco will cut him off.*

Kate raced through the house, finding that her assumptions were right. There was a very faint aroma of pot, mixed with the smell of spilled beer. As she ran through the kitchen, she entered a hallway that led back toward two bedrooms. There, at the end of the hall, a back door was still wobbling in its frame from someone having just run out of it. She sprinted to the door and pushed it open, ready to attack if necessary. But she had seen the fear in Jeremy's eyes. He was not going to attack at all; he had every intention of outrunning them. And if he made it to the woods no more than fifteen feet away from the back door, he might very well be able to do it.

She saw him, streaking toward the tree line, but then she also saw DeMarco. She was closing in from the left side of the house. She wasn't bothering to draw her weapon or to scream for Jeremy to stop. Kate was astounded by just how fast her partner was, barreling after Jeremy at a speed that easily bested the teenager's.

She caught up to him just as Jeremy had reached the first line of trees that led into the forest. DeMarco reached out, grabbed his shoulder, and spun him around to face her. In doing so, Jeremy ended up spinning like a top, making an entire three-hundred-sixty-degree spin before losing his balance and falling to the ground.

Kate hurried down a shaky set of back steps and joined DeMarco, helping her to handcuff Jeremy Branch.

"When you run," Kate said, "it makes us think you have something to hide. And you also just made our choice easier. We'll be talking to you down at the station."

Jeremy Branch had nothing to say to this. He panted heavily as DeMarco hauled him to his feet with his hands cuffed behind his back. He looked bewildered and out of sorts as they walked him to their car. And when he looked nervously back toward the trailer, Kate was pretty sure she'd find enough suspicious evidence to get

Jeremy and his brother in quite a bit of trouble, even aside from the disappearance of Mercy Fuller.

***

The search inside the house did not take long. While DeMarco remained outside, Kate scoured the place and within fifteen minutes, had found more than enough to get the Branch brothers into a lot of trouble.

Half a pound of cocaine had been found in one of the bedrooms, along with half a dozen ecstasy pills. In the other bedroom, there were several plastic baggies of pot, another dozen ecstasy pills, and a few containers of prescription pain medicine. The real kicker had come when Kate had found a small black notebook beneath the bed of the second bedroom. It looked to be a tally book of sorts, recording who owed money and for what.

She also figured out that the first bedroom she'd checked was Jeremy Branch's. She knew this because of a rather provocative picture sitting on his bedside, featuring himself and Mercy Fuller, who was mostly undressed. But she could find no journals, no laptop, nothing that might lend clues as to his involvement in her disappearance or the deaths of her parents.

She did find one thing of note, though. Something that answered at least one question. In the small bathroom just off of Jeremy's bedroom, Kate found a new travel-sized toothpaste, female deodorant, and a new miniature-sized toothbrush. Apparently, Mercy had bought those things to keep here, trying to cover up any traces of having been physical with a boy before she went home.

She headed back outside, wading through the tall grass for the car. "All of the travel-sized stuff is in Jeremy's bathroom. Apparently, Mercy was keeping it all here."

"That's...cute, I guess?"

"Or a bit obsessive," Kate suggested as she got behind the wheel. "Also, we now know one of the reasons he ran."

From the back, Jeremy spoke up, his voice panicked and ringed with fear. "All of that stuff is my brother's."

"So he was just keeping some of it in your room, then?"

"Yeah, he sells it and...and..."

"Save your wind for the station," Kate said. "Truth be told, the drugs are only secondary right now."

"I had nothing to do with Mercy or her parents," he said. "I swear."

23

"I hope not," Kate said as she started the car forward. "But I guess we'll just have to wait and see."

CHAPTER FIVE

This time, when they entered the Deton Police Station, the large desk at the front of the bullpen was occupied by a woman who looked like she had been planted there and had never left. She was easily sixty years of age and when she looked up at Kate, DeMarco, and Jeremy Branch, she gave a well-rehearsed smile. When she realized what was going on, though, the smile faded and she was all business.

"You the agents?" she asked.

"Yes ma'am," DeMarco said. "Where can we park Mr. Branch here?"

"The interrogation room for right now. I'll get the sheriff on the phone and let him know you're here. Follow me."

The older woman led them alongside the bullpen, down the same hallway Barnes had led them down earlier. She opened the door to the second room on the right. It looked pretty much the same as the one they had met Officer Foster in earlier in the day. There was an old scarred desk with one chair parked on either side.

"Sit down," DeMarco said, giving Jeremy a light push in the direction of the table.

Jeremy did as he was asked, not resisting at all. When his butt was in the seat, he folded his handcuffed hands in front of him and stared at them.

"What was the relationship between you and Mercy Fuller like?" Kate asked.

"I barely knew her."

"I saw a picture in your bedroom that says otherwise."

"What would you say if I told you she was that...well, that *friendly* to most guys?"

"I'd say that's a pretty daring accusation to point at someone. Especially in a town like this one, about a girl who just lost both of her parents."

Jeremy sighed and gave a shrug. His nonchalance was aggravating Kate but she did her best to remain professional.

"I told you...I don't know *anything* about that family."

"You're lying," Kate said. "And here's the thing. You can keep lying, but this is a small town, kid. I can unwrap your lie pretty easily. And if I do find out you're lying to me, *then* we'll start digging into the drugs. Maybe find some of the people your not-so-bright brother has listed in that black notebook under his bed. Maybe tell them that you told us where to find the book."

Jeremy's eyes widened at this thought and he started to shift in his seat. Kate also wondered if there might be a card to play in terms of his older brother. She wondered which of the two might crack under pressure first.

But apparently, she was not going to have to go that route. She could practically see the moment when Jeremy Branch decided that his own self-preservation was the most important thing.

"Fine, I know her. But we weren't like dating or anything. We just hooked up every now and then."

"So it was a sexual relationship?"

"Yes. And that's about all it was."

"Did you not care that she was fifteen?"

"I kind of did. I figured I'd just break it off with her when I turned eighteen. So I wouldn't get in trouble, you know?"

"When was the last time you saw her?" DeMarco asked.

"Maybe a week or so ago."

"Did she come to your place?"

"Yes. We had this sort of blueprint. When she wanted to come over, she'd text me and I'd pick her up over on Waterlick Road. She'd tell her folks she was going to a friend's house and I'd pick her up and we'd go back to my place."

"How long had this been going on?" Kate asked.

"Four or five months. But look, I know it sounds dirty or whatever, but I really don't know her all that well. It was just sex. That's all. I was her first…and she was sort of curious, you know? She wasn't like sex crazy or anything, but we met up a lot."

"I thought you said she was *friendly* with most guys," DeMarco said.

His only response to this apparent lie in an attempt to save face was a shrug.

"What about her parents?" Kate asked. "What can you tell me about them?"

"Nothing. I knew who her dad was, you know? I mean, it's a small town. You sort of know everyone. Plus, she always used to joke that if her dad found out we were fu—having sex," he said, apparently not finding it appropriate to drop other terminology in front of two female agents, "he'd kill me."

"And did you believe her?"

"I don't know. But I guess. A guy never really wants to think about the father of the girl he's sleeping with finding out. I didn't

26

know what to think about her parents. I mean, she hated them. Like *loathed* them, you know?"

"She did?"

"Based on the way she talked about them, yeah I think so. If I can…"

He stopped here and seemed to think about something for a minute. He then looked at Kate and DeMarco as if he were trying to figure out his boundaries.

"What is it?" Kate asked.

"Look. Yeah, it was messed it up that we slept with each other like twenty times or so and I didn't know her all that well. But I always thought it was sort of weird to hear her talk about her parents like that."

"Like what?"

Before he could answer, there was a knock on the door. Sheriff Barnes opened it and poked his head inside. There was a quick look exchanged between Barnes and Jeremy, making Kate think this was probably not the first time Jeremy had spent time in this room.

"Jeremy Branch?" he asked. "What the hell is he doing here?"

"You want to tell him or should we?" DeMarco asked. She gave Jeremy a few seconds and when he did not start talking, she brought Barnes up to speed. "He was sleeping with Mercy Fuller…as recently as last week. He was just telling us how he found it strange that Mercy would speak so negatively about her parents. How she hated them."

"Sleeping with her?" Barnes asked. "Damn, son…how old are you?"

"Seventeen. I don't turn eighteen for another month."

"Go on," Kate said, redirecting him back toward the point. "Tell us what kind of stuff Mercy would say about her parents."

"Just how they never let her do anything. How they didn't trust her. I think she had some really bad beef with her mother because I know there were at least two or three times where she something like 'I just want to kill that bitch.' She *hated* her mom."

"Did she ever talk about the relationship between her parents?" Kate asked.

"No. She rarely talked about them. She'd vent for a while, get sort of mad, and then that's usually when we'd have sex. I just…I don't know. I never thought she'd actually do it."

"Do what?" Barnes asked.

Jeremy then looked up at them as if they had missed the entire point. "Seriously? Look…like I said. She seems sort of innocent, aside from being sort of a nympho, but if you're looking for her parents' killer…find her. I guarantee you Mercy killed her parents and then just split town."

CHAPTER SIX

So far, no one had actually taken the seat on the opposite side of the desk; Kate, DeMarco, and Barnes were all still standing. But when Jeremy made such a bold statement, Sheriff Barnes walked slowly to the chair and sat down directly across from the teenager. There was a mixture of sadness and fury in his eyes as he pointed an accusatory finger in Jeremy's face.

"I've been sheriff in this town for sixteen years. I knew Wendy and Alvin Fuller quite well. And as far as I know, Mercy Fuller was a stand-up young woman. Certainly not a trouble-making piece of shit like you. So if you're going to sit here and make such an accusation, I suggest you have a damn good story to back it up."

Jeremy nodded, clearly very scared now. "I do."

Barnes folded his arms, leaned back in the chair, and sneered at Jeremy. As Jeremy started to talk, his eyes never left Barnes. If Kate had to venture a guess, he was probably concerned that Barnes might launch himself across the table at any moment to strangle him.

"We'd been fooling around for maybe three or four weeks the first time she ever mentioned running away from home. She asked me if I'd go with her. Said she wanted to go somewhere to North Carolina or something like that. I made fun of her because I didn't see the point in moving just one state away, you know? Plus, I didn't like her like that. My brother joked with me how the first guy a girl sleeps with, she gets obsessed. I guess she sort of did. Anyway, there was no way I was going to run away with her. But the way she talked about it...you could tell she had actually thought about it."

"Do you think she wanted to run away because of just how much she disliked her parents?" Kate asked.

"I guess. I mean, it's the only real reason I could think of that would make her want to leave home. I mean...my parents are assholes, too. But I didn't run away or nothing."

"No," Barnes said. "You just moved two miles away into your older brother's trailer. Maybe Mercy didn't have an option like that."

"Still," Kate said, making sure Barnes didn't take them too far off-topic. "Are you certain she was being for real when she spoke of running away? Not just filling your head with fantasies so you'd stay with her?"

"No. But she kept talking about how her mother would go crazy trying to find her—not because she'd actually *want* to find her but because she'd feel like Mercy got one over on her by running away."

"Do you know if there was any abuse in her home?" DeMarco asked.

"I don't think so. Not recently, anyway. She did tell me one time about how her mother hauled off and just hit her right in the face when she was like eleven or twelve."

"And you swear she never actually came out and said she was *going* to kill them?" Kate asked.

"A few times, she did. She would say 'I can't wait to kill them.' And then she talked about whether she'd do it with a knife or a gun. She really liked talking about it. But I told her to shut up. When me and Mercy got together, it was just for the sex. And I didn't want to hear about her thinking about killing her parents before we got down to it, you know?"

Kate considered it all as Jeremy stopped talking and looked around at all three of them. He had lied about Mercy being promiscuous. Kate wondered if everything else he had said was also a lie.

She leaned down close to a still-sitting Sheriff Barnes and whispered into his ear: "Can we speak outside for a moment?"

He nodded and got up, practically having to tear his eyes away from Jeremy. He didn't just walk out of the room—he *stormed* out. Before he said a word to Kate or DeMarco as they followed him, he went straight into his office. He held the door open for them and closed it when they were both inside.

Right away, he said: "Shit."

"You think he's telling the truth?" Kate asked.

"I think there are enough truthful tidbits in his story to make it believable. That little story about Wendy Fuller punching Mercy…that really happened. Mercy called the police. She wasn't sad when she did it, either. It was about five years ago, but I remember it well. She was vindictive about it. Wanted to make sure her mom got into trouble. But in the end, all it took was a little sit-down with the family and all was well. Wendy had a drinking problem back then. From what I understand, she's been clean and sober for about two years now. As for this shit with Mercy hating her parents with a passion…I just don't know for sure."

30

"Everything he's telling us is the exact opposite of what Anne Pettus said. She said Mercy loved her parents...that they got along really well."

"Here's where I get stuck," Barnes said. "Jeremy Branch and his older brother are nothing but troublemakers. I've busted his brother twice for possession of drugs and once for lewd conduct in the back of his truck out on the back roads. As for Jeremy, I've had him in here just once—for petty larceny. But I always figured it would be just a matter of time before he became more of a regular."

"Would he have any need to lie about Mercy potentially being the killer?" DeMarco asked.

"I just don't know. But...it makes a lot of sense, right? Girl gets fed up with her parents, kills them, and then runs away."

Kate nodded. She recalled her own imagined scenario of Mercy approaching her unsuspecting parents and killing them both before the second one she killed was even sure of what was happening.

"How long has Jeremy been living with his brother?" Kate asked.

"I don't know. For good, maybe a year or so. Even before that, though, he would live with his brother off and on. His brother is Randy Branch—a twenty-five-year-old permanent screw-up. Their parents divorced about ten years ago. Randy got his own place as soon as he could, that miserable old double-wide out on the edge of the woods. For a while, I think Jeremy bounced back and forth between his parents but then their mother moved in with family down in Alabama. After that, I think their father just sort of stopped caring."

"But he lives around here?"

"Yeah, out on Waterlick Road."

"Any idea if Jeremy ever stays with him at all?"

"Not personally. I hear rumors, though. And one of those rumors is that Randy has these pretty raunchy parties. Orgies, I guess, I don't know. And he doesn't let Jeremy hang around. So from what I hear, the weekends he has these parties, Jeremy stays with his old man." He paused here and then, almost skeptically, added: "You don't think it was Mercy?"

"You *do*?"

He shrugged. "I don't want to believe it, but it's starting to look like it. If I'm being honest, it's a conclusion I started to consider even before you showed up."

"Let's hold Jeremy here for a bit longer," Kate said. "In the meantime, do you think you could have someone trace down the address and contact information of Jeremy's father?"

31

"Yeah, I'll get Foster on it," he said, reaching for his phone. "He'll be glad to be able to add a little more information to his case files."

Kate and DeMarco stepped outside of the office, walking back toward the bullpen area. Speaking under her breath, DeMarco asked: "Do you think Jeremy Branch is telling the truth?"

"I just don't know. His story certainly adds up and connects a lot of dots. But I also know that with all the drugs I found in that house, he has every reason in the world to cover his ass and get the attention off of him."

"I can't help but wonder if *he* was in on the deaths himself," DeMarco said. "An older guy, wanting to keep a younger girl under lock and key. If she truly hated her parents and he was crazy enough, wouldn't he be a suspect?"

It was a promising train of thought, one that Kate had considered herself. She had not ruled it out, hoping that a visit to Jeremy's father's house would give them some more information.

"Agents?"

They both turned to see Barnes coming out of his office. He handed a slip of paper to Kate and nodded. "That's the address for Floyd Branch. Fair warning, though…he can be a bit of a bastard. Badges and all that don't really bother him."

"It's the middle of the day," Kate said. "Are you even sure he'll be home?"

"Yeah. He works on small engines and stuff like that out of his garage." Barnes checked his watched and smiled. "It's just about three thirty, so I bet you just about anything that he's already started drinking. If I were you, I'd head out that way soon…before he gets hammered. Want some backup? He's kind of a hillbilly. I don't know how else to put that. He's going to see two women he doesn't know and not take you seriously."

"Sounds lovely," Kate said. "Sure. Come on along, Sheriff. The more, the merrier."

She honestly didn't believe in that little tidbit but she did know the sort of man Barnes was describing. She'd seen a lot of it in the South, especially. There were some rural areas where men had simply not caught up to the world, not only disrespecting women but unable to see them as equals…even when they were carrying a badge and a gun.

They left the station together, heading for the bureau's rental that DeMarco had driven in from DC. *Wow, that was just this morning,* she thought.

It made her think of Allen and the plans he had tried making for them—a quick escape away to the mountains to drink wine, sleep in, and other things in a bed that weren't exactly *sleeping*.

And while she was still rather down about missing out on such a thing, she was also willing to admit that she was just as excited right now, with a case unfolding in front of her. She still had some work to do in keeping a proper balance between her personal life and her unique bureau schedule but for now, she felt that she was exactly where she needed to be.

CHAPTER SEVEN

Floyd Branch's property was a living embodiment of all Southern stereotypes. As DeMarco pulled the car into the lightly graveled driveway, the lyrics to about a dozen country songs all presented themselves in the form of Floyd Branch's trailer, yard, and scattered possessions.

The grass was only slightly better than what they had previously seen at Jeremy's place. Portions of the lawn around the trailer had at least been mown, dead spots showing through here and there. The mower itself—an old riding mower with a rusted hood, was parked directly beside a shed to the back of the house. Two junked trucks—one completely missing its back end—sat on concrete blocks next to it. Beside the shed was a weak-looking dog pen, made primarily of wooden planks, a few metal poles, and what looked like chicken wire. As DeMarco parked the car and they all got out, two pit bulls inside the pen started to make ungodly noises, something between a bark and a roar.

Kate, DeMarco, and Barnes had taken only a few steps away from the car before a middle-aged gaunt-looking man came out of the shed. He carried a broom with him, looking angrily toward the pen and cursing at the dogs. He then saw that he had visitors. His anger dropped and he tossed the broom back into the shed as if embarrassed by it.

"Hey there, Sheriff."

"Floyd, hey yourself. How are you today?"

"Okay, I guess. Working on an old dirt bike motor for the Wells family. The bike is older'n hell. Seems like a waste to me, but he already paid, so…"

He stopped here, clearly distracted as he tried to take in the two women on either side of Barnes. He looked both shaken and slightly excited. Not because there were women on his property, but because it was something unexpected—something new and out of the ordinary.

"Floyd, these two ladies are with the FBI. They'd like to ask you some questions."

"FBI? What the hell for? I ain't done nothing."

"Oh, I don't expect you have," Barnes said. "But tell me, Floyd: when was the last time you spoke with Jeremy?"

34

"Ah shit, what's he done?"

"We don't know yet," Kate said. "Maybe nothing at all. We've come here to find out for sure."

"He's been involved with Mercy Fuller," Barnes explained. "Alvin and Wendy's daughter. We have him down at the station for questioning. I thought you should know that."

"What? Damn, Sheriff." Floyd shrugged and shook his head. "It's no wonder, though. That boy never tells me anything. It's probably been about three weeks since I saw him. He stayed here a few nights while Randy was tending to his own stuff. But I'm pretty sure he came by for a little while a few nights ago when I was out at the bar. He left the light on in his room. He comes over here sometimes to watch movies. Porn, mostly, I think. Little weirdo."

"And he never mentioned Mercy Wheeler?" Kate asked.

"No. Hell, we barely even spoke at all. Talked football, some. How the Redskins are going to shit. He asked about his ma but I wasn't about to have that conversation, you know?" He paused here, as if suddenly struck but a thought. "Damn. The Fullers? I heard about what happened to them. Did Mercy get killed, too?"

"No," Barnes said. "In fact, she's gone missing."

"We spoke to Jeremy about his involvement with her," Kate said. "He told us that Mercy didn't like her parents and he's suggesting that Mercy had something to do with their murders."

"I don't know why he'd lie about it," Floyd said. He did not sound offended that they were making such an accusation. In fact, he seemed rather detached from the whole situation, like he simply didn't care at all. "Were they dating?"

"Jeremy says it was just a physical relationship," DeMarco said. "But he also said that she would confide in him—telling him how she hated her parents. How she wanted to kill them."

"Forgive me for asking such a dumb question," Floyd said, "but why are you here? Hell, Sheriff Barnes...you probably know Jeremy better than I do."

"Does he have a room here?" Kate asked.

"Yeah. Last one down the hallway."

"Would you allow us to look around it?"

Floyd hesitated here, unsure of how to answer. He looked to Barnes, as if for help or backup of some kind.

"You got something in that trailer I might not approve of, Floyd?" Barnes asked.

Instead of answering outright, Floyd asked: "Just Jeremy's room. Right?"

"For now," Barnes said with some skepticism. "Thanks, Floyd."

Barnes escorted Kate and DeMarco to the trailer. As they walked up the rickety porch, Kate looked back out at Floyd Branch. He was walking back into his shed, seemingly unaffected by the exchange.

"He wasn't nearly as bad as you were letting on," Kate said.

"Apparently he's getting a late start on drinking today."

They walked inside the trailer and Kate was surprised by what she saw. She had been expecting it to be in a state of disrepair, cluttered and messy. But Floyd apparently owned very little, including anything that could consist of clutter. The place was fairly clean, though it had the same sort of smell Kate had experienced at his son's trailer earlier: stale beer and something slightly pungent that was probably old pot smoke.

The hallway was thin and only held three rooms: a bedroom, a bathroom, and a smaller bedroom near the back. Kate and DeMarco entered Jeremy's room while Barnes hung back.

"I'm here for any support you need," he said. "But there's barely enough room for the two of you in there, much less the three of us."

He was right. The room was very small, taken up mostly by a twin mattress sitting on the floor and an old desk that was piled up with DVDs and CDs. A small television and dusty DVD player sat on the floor at the foot of the mattress, their wires and cables snaking around the floor. A cell phone sat on top of the television, hooked to a charger that ran to a multi-outlet adapter that also powered the TV, DVD player, and the small box fan in the window.

Kate picked the phone up. It was an iPhone, about three models behind the most current. When she pressed the Home button, the screen instantly popped up. No password needed. The home screen showed only a few apps: a few games, settings, photos, and clock. She figured this was just a passed down phone, one with no service but still used for games. She had a few friends who had eased their older kids into owning a cell phone this same way. Before gifting them with a full-service phone, they had allowed their kids to have a hand-me-down without full services, capable of only texting selected users and playing games that did not require Wi-Fi.

Behind her, DeMarco was flipping through the movies. "Floyd really wasn't kidding about his son watching porn back here. Half of these are amateur porn titles. The other half are Cinemax-style sex stuff."

Kate kept looking through the phone. She opened up photos and found that it was packed. Some were of girls, all partying. A few were topless. A few were kissing one another, the expressions on their faces a clear indication that they were wasted. There were a few videos of these events, all rather brief. She slid right past these until she came to one that was just under five minutes long. In the thumbnail of the video, she saw Mercy Fuller's face.

She pressed Play and it took her less than three seconds to understand what she was seeing before she shut it off. In the video, Mercy was lying on her back, being videoed from just above her. The director was apparently Jeremy, filming while having some fairly rough sex with her. It was not forced, if the sounds coming from Mercy were any indication.

"Jesus," Kate said, sliding out of Photos.

"What was that?" DeMarco asked.

"Proof that Jeremy Branch was telling the truth about at least one thing: they were definitely having sex."

Kate saw that while the phone in her hand had no access to Contacts—it did not need it, as calls were impossible from it—she did see that there were a few text threads. She opened up the messages and saw only three conversations. One was with a contact that had been titled BRO and the texts made it obvious that they were to and from his brother, Randy. One of the others was to a guy named Chuck and the entire thread was about which celebrities they would like to have sex with and why.

The third message thread was from a contact Jeremy had titled BOOTY CALL. The little picture above the name was Mercy Fuller, head tilted and making a kissing face.

"I might have hit the jackpot over here," Kate said.

DeMarco came over and they both started reading through the thread. It was quite long, spanning back over the last several months. The vast majority of it consisted of long drawn-out messages from Mercy with very short, often only one-word responses from Jeremy. The more they read, the clearer it became that Jeremy Branch had been lying to them. He may have been truthful about the nature of their relationship, but the picture he had painted of Mercy and her parents was totally untrue.

And that raised a very important question.

If he was lying about that, what else was he hiding?

CHAPTER EIGHT

Kate walked back into the interrogation room as calmly as she could. DeMarco was with her and while she, too, was irritated, she had agreed to let Kate run the bulk of this second interrogation. Similarly, Barnes was also hanging back, fielding a few calls about other local interests in his office.

Kate sat down across from Jeremy, her expression blank. She could already tell that Jeremy was nervous, his eyes shifting back and forth between Kate, DeMarco, and the surface of the desk between them.

"The good news is that you're a very convincing liar," Kate said. "The bad news is, you aren't particularly bright."

Jeremy said nothing. He continued to sit there, looking dumbfounded, waiting to see where Kate took the conversation next. Kate took the old cell phone out of her pocket and placed it on the desk.

"You left this in your bedroom at your father's place," she said. "Stored away with all of your porn. We noticed that some of your own amateur stuff is also on this phone. Of course, I can tell by the look on your face that you know there is more than just incriminating pictures on here."

Jeremy still remained silent. He was not being defiant; he was simply at a loss. He had nothing to say. So Kate went on, assuming that if she kept pushing, he'd end up talking.

"There are very long conversations between you and Mercy Fuller on this phone," Kate said. "Several times during those conversations, she talks about her parents—her father in particular. In one of those conversations, she goes so far as to say that she likely has the coolest father in the world, the exception being his taste in music. She also, at one point, tells you that she'd like for you to meet her parents, even if only for you to taste how delicious her mother's homemade lasagna is. She also talks about being excited for college and how the only real thing that makes her afraid to leave home when college time comes around is leaving her parents behind. Now…that does not sound like a girl who hated her parents and not *at all* like a girl who was planning to kill her parents."

38

Slowly, Jeremy reached for the phone. Kate promptly grabbed it back up and got to her feet. "Why'd you lie to us, Jeremy? Are you hiding something?"

"No," he said. "I just wanted you running in circles for coming after me. The law in this stupid county is always after my brother. Gave my old man a hell of a hard time back in the day, too."

"Trying to stick it to the law?" Kate asked. "You really *aren't* very bright, are you? This is not you just screwing with some local investigation, wasting the time of the cops. This is interfering with a federal case. And based on all of the drugs I found in your brother's house, your little act—your bullshit story—could get you in a lot of trouble."

Jeremy looked genuinely scared now. It had not taken much and the way he was shifting between emotions—from prideful to stubborn to scared—told her all she needed to know about him. He had lived his life wanting to appease someone—probably his brother or father—and was seldom thinking for himself. And now here he was with his tough-guy act crumbling before him, looking down a path that could lead him to some very serious trouble.

"Look…I don't know anything about what happened to her."

"Forgive me if I don't believe you," Kate said.

"I swear, I don't! I've done some messed up shit, but I would never kidnap someone. And I wouldn't k-k-kill someone."

His stutter and the glistening of tears in the corners of his eyes made Kate believe that he was right. No matter how good of a liar he was, it was very hard to fake that sincere sort of emotion.

"Where is Mercy, Jeremy?"

"I swear, I don't know!" He slapped at his own face as a tear trailed down his cheek.

"When was the last time you saw her?" DeMarco asked.

"Last week. It was just for a little while. Usually we at least talk and hang out a bit before I take her back to Waterlick Road. But that last time…"

"What? It's okay," Kate said. "No need to be modest on us now."

"Well, she was really into it. It was quick and sort of rough and when we were done, she said she wanted to go home. Right away."

"And that was unlike her?"

"Yeah. She usually liked to cuddle up and talk when we were done. Maybe smoke a little weed."

Kate waited for about thirty seconds before she tried again. She leaned across the table and, as menacingly as she could muster without actually accusing him, she asked: "Where is she, Jeremy?"

"I don't know!"

"How do I know you're not lying to us about this, too?"

"I'm not! I'm telling you the truth!"

Kate crossed her arms, stared him down for a moment, and then headed for the door. When she walked out, DeMarco followed closely behind her.

"It's not him," Kate said quietly.

"I'm getting that vibe, too," DeMarco agreed.

"You feel like staying overnight in Deton?"

"It wouldn't be on my bucket list, if that's what you mean. But I'd rather stay here than drive back to DC and repeat it all over again tomorrow morning."

"I think we need to have Sheriff Barnes hold Jeremy for a while. The longer he's here, the more he'll start to worry about his brother. The more he'll start to worry about his own fate. If he *is* hiding something else, time will pull it out of him. Besides…based on his lies, the drugs, some of the stuff on his phone, and his relationship with Mercy, there's plenty to hold him on."

"Maybe we should get one last meeting in before the day ends. Get Foster back in here and go over what we know."

"Good idea. And while we're doing that, maybe some more truths will come tumbling out of Jeremy Branch."

But really, she thought Jeremy had been as truthful as he could be. While he showed no real remorse for the disappearance of the underage girl he was sleeping with, the fear she'd seen in his eyes made her believe he'd given them everything he had. And at the end of the day, it hadn't been all that much.

***

At 6:15, a very small meeting was held in the conference room. It consisted of Kate, DeMarco, Barnes, and Foster. Barnes had considered bringing one more officer in on it but decided not to. The Deton police force consisted of six active-duty cops and, as Barnes had explained, Foster was the only one Barnes trusted not to blab about the case all over town.

"So you went out to Floyd's place?" Foster asked.

"We did," Kate said. "That's where we found the phone."

"I assume Floyd did absolutely nothing about the fact that his youngest son was spending time at the station?"

"Hardly," Barnes said. "I've already explained to the agents the type of stand-up father Floyd Branch is. He won't be a factor in whatever happens to Jeremy."

"That's what we need to figure out," Kate said. "I don't think Jeremy is guilty. Not of Mercy's disappearance and not the murders. If he had something to do with her disappearance, I don't see him so casually answering the door for us the way he did this morning. And if he killed the Fullers, there's no way he would stick around town."

"Maybe that's exactly what he'd want you to think," Foster said.

"I've considered that."

"Frankly," DeMarco said, "based on what we've seen and been told about Jeremy and his family, I simply don't see him being motivated enough to kill anyone. There's also the fact that he really had no real reason to commit the murders."

"Well, he *is* having sex with their fifteen-year-old daughter. And, as you said, by his own admission, she was taking drugs with him."

"Let's not forget, though," Kate said, "that we don't have a single shred of evidence that points to him. Just a sexual relationship with Mercy Fuller."

Barnes let out a deep sigh and massaged his temples. "This is a damned mess. I'm hearing out on the streets that people are assuming Mercy Fuller killed her parents and just ran away. Why people would assume that before they assumed that some killer did away with her parents and then took her as some sort of a prize is beyond me."

"Can you think of *anyone* local who might be capable of such a thing?" Kate asked.

"That's just the thing. I can't think of a single one. Look, I'm not blind to what Deton and most of the county looks like. Poor old country people. Not very educated. Borderline poor. A place where people like Floyd Branch and his sons are pretty much the norm. They might lead sketchy lives, but they are, for the most part, pretty quiet. We don't have real troublemakers here."

"Outside of seventeen-year-old guys having lots of sex and drugs with underage girls," Kate said. She regretted it the moment she said it. There was the slightest flinch in both Barnes and Foster as she basically insulted their town.

"This was probably an outsider," DeMarco said. "Someone passing through town or, maybe more realistically, someone meeting up with a local dealer like Randy Branch and sticking around to start some trouble."

"Could be," Kate said. "Most murders in small towns end up being the work of someone not local."

"So that makes the net a lot wider," Barnes said. "Great."

"In the meantime," Kate said, getting to her feet. "Is there any way we could get files on any arrests for violent activity in Deton and the surrounding towns over the course of the last five years or so?"

"I can get that together for you," Foster said. "But I'm afraid it won't be much."

They adjourned their little meeting, Kate deciding not to pay another visit to Jeremy Branch before she left. The longer he sat in the interrogation room with his thoughts, the better chance they had of him revealing something else.

But she was pretty sure that avenue was all used up.

And she was also sure that if they didn't find another one soon, Mercy Fuller might never be seen again—alive or dead.

CHAPTER NINE

The floor was hard and cold. She'd been sitting on it for days and it had made her backside go numb. Her back was aching, too. There was nothing comfortable about the place. It was dark, it smelled bad, and it felt like a coffin.

Maybe it is my coffin, she thought. *Maybe this is where I die.*

This thought made her want to start bawling again, but she was too tired to cry. She doubted there was enough moisture in her body to produce any more tears.

Although the space was much larger than an actual coffin, she could not ignore the way the place made her think of a grave. She wasn't sure how long she had been here because of the darkness. She had no idea if it was day or night. She could have been here for maybe two days…or maybe five. Maybe longer. She had no idea.

Whoever had placed her here had taken meager precautions for her. There was a small cooler against the back wall, something that had taken her forever to open because of the absolute darkness. Inside, she had found a six-pack of soda in ice. Beside the cooler, she'd found a thin rectangular box. Upon opening it, she found cheese crackers.

She'd snacked on them even though she had no appetite. And already, she had finished two of the sodas. She'd had to pee and, in a humiliating moment, had done so in the back corner of her pitch-black prison.

On a few different occasions, she had occupied her mind by doing a study of her environment while trapped in the dark. She had to. It was the only thing preventing her from curling up in the back and just waiting to die. It not only gave her something to do but it gave her just a glimmer of hope—a hope that told her if she could better understand where she was, maybe she could figure a way out.

She did it again now, needing to move her legs and keep her blood flowing. There was the floor, made of what she assumed was metal. She reached up, standing on her toes, and could not touch the ceiling. She figured that meant that whatever weird place she was in, it was at least seven or eight feet tall.

She started taking steps from the back of the wall, which felt like it was made of aluminum, knowing that when she made eight steps, she'd come to another wall. Sure enough, eight steps brought her to another aluminum wall. She pushed gently against it. Maybe it wasn't aluminum. Maybe just hollow metal. Maybe…

She almost drew her hand back to thump on it—to see what it was made of. But the last thing she wanted to do was to attract the man that she supposed had brought her here. She really couldn't remember how she had gotten here. She remembered sitting in the kitchen and hearing her parents scream. Her father had even yelled at her to run but the sentence had been cut short. Still, she *had* run—because of the gunshots. She'd had her phone in her hand and had started to dial the police when she ran into something on her way out of the back door.

And that was the last thing she remembered. She had a very fleeting memory of scenery passing by a darkened car window, but that was all. After that, she had opened her eyes to this dark place.

She walked to the wall to her right and did her little counting-by-steps procedure again. From front to back, the place she was trapped inside was eight heel-to-toe steps. Walking from side to side in the same manner allowed her only five steps. She outstretched both of her arms as wide as she could and found that she could not touch the sides.

So this thing… it's something like eight feet by five feet. Right?

She knew she was lousy with measurements. But at least she could hold that concrete information in her mind. At least she had *some* type of knowledge in this—

"Is my little pet moving around again?"

His voice came from somewhere beyond the darkness. It was the third time he had spoken to her. He had an almost cheerful voice. It made him sound like he might be pretty young, but she couldn't be sure.

She did not respond. Hearing his voice, she slunk back to the farthest corner of that dark place and cowered.

"You can talk back to me, if you want," he said. "But like I said before… if you scream for help, no one will hear you. And if you try it, I'll hurt you. But in a way that's going to make me feel *plenty* good. You understand?"

"Please," she muttered. "Please let me out. I'll…I'll do whatever you want."

"I don't doubt it," he said dryly. "But I can't let you out. Not just yet."

"Please…"

She couldn't help it. She started crying then. It was just as well, because her captor did not respond to her. She wondered if he was standing out there, enjoying her pleading. Finally, he spoke up again.

"Do you understand what I said?" he asked again.

She thought she did. She thought she understood perfectly. And there was something in his voice that made her believe him. Sure, it was cheerful but there was something almost childlike in it—something that made him sound crazy.

And it was that crazy timbre to his voice that made Mercy Fuller feel that she didn't have much time—that he may decide to just go ahead and kill her at any moment.

CHAPTER TEN

Kate had never been much of a drinker. She'd have a glass of wine here and there and whenever she did, she thought of her mother. Her mother had enjoyed a single glass of white wine every night, just after dinner. One glass; no more, no less. She'd have a few more on special occasions like birthdays or anniversaries, but even then, she was very selective.

She thought of her mother as she sat at the small bar that sat just off of Deton's only motel—a sloppy-looking Best Western. She sipped on a glass of wine as DeMarco enjoyed a beer roughly the color of a moonless midnight.

"Have you noticed all of the locals banding together?" DeMarco asked. "All these locals, trying to help with finding this one girl."

"I have," Kate said. "I overheard two officers talking in the station, about this newly retired man who is heading it up. He's had people out in the woods, looking for anything that might help."

"And God knows Barnes can use all the help he can get. I think he's a good enough leader, but the force itself…"

"They're doing their best," Kate said. "But I'm not sure that's quite enough."

They fell into silence then. Kate felt rather bad, sitting here with a drink while there was a missing girl out there. But she knew there was not much she could do right now. Sometimes a case came down to a moment when there was nothing to do but wait.

"How's your granddaughter?" DeMarco asked.

"Crawling. Can you believe it? She literally started just before I got the call about this case."

"Jeez…already?"

"Yeah. That's the thing about kids. They grow up so damned fast. It seems like it's going even faster now that I have a grandkid."

DeMarco smiled and took a sip from her beer. "Please don't take this the wrong way…but just based on how I know you, I find it very hard to believe you're a grandmother."

"Why's that?"

"Because you're such a badass. You don't think of women like you as having grandkids."

46

"Thanks...I think. How about you? Anything new going on in your life?"

"Sort of. But it's a little embarrassing."

"That makes me want to hear it even more."

"Well...I sort of write in my spare time. I have for a while. Nothing serious, just a hobby, you know? Anyway...I sold my first short story a few weeks ago."

"Hey, that's great!"

"It's just a small online journal thing. Thirty bucks for it."

"What's it about?"

"It's, um...well, it's sort of R-rated. Actually, it might be closer to NC-17. Lots of sex. Lots of women."

Kate chuckled and nodded her head. "Hey, whatever sells, right? Now, is this piece a reflective piece on your life?"

It might have been the first time Kate had ever seen DeMarco uncomfortable. She took a longer sip from her beer and gave a small nod. "I'm actually *dating* someone now. More than just casually seeing. It's nice."

"That's fantastic. How long?"

"About two months. She's an interesting one. And I know that because when she met my parents two weeks ago, that was the verbiage my mother used. *Interesting*."

"So—and forgive me for asking—but have your parents always been okay with you being gay?"

"Mom fought it for a while, but not for very long," DeMarco said. "Keep in mind, I dropped this bombshell on them when I was only fourteen. I was sixteen when she finally came around."

"And does Director Duran know?"

"Yeah. I told him before I was even hired." She laughed here and shook her head. "When you were coming up in the bureau, it was still taboo, huh?"

"Not taboo. But I think if it *did* come up in an interview or something like that, it would be a topic of discussion behind closed doors before a decision would be made."

"Man, we've come a long way, huh?"

"We have. I wonder, though...was it always easy for you? I may be way off the mark here, but you don't seem to wear your sexuality on your sleeve. You keep it private. It's like you're accustomed to it, like you're comfortable in it. Has it always been like that?"

A look came over DeMarco's face that Kate thought might be one of appreciation. And as she began to speak, it again made Kate wonder how DeMarco viewed her. As only a co-worker? As a friend? Maybe as a secondary kind of mother-figure? Or all of the above?

For the next several minutes, DeMarco told a large part of her story. How she discovered she was homosexual the first time she kissed a boy, in some lazy form of Seven Minutes in Heaven when she was fourteen. She'd wasted no time telling her parents, instantly going to them for advice. She detailed a few awkward months as her parents came to terms with it, wrapping up with a touching moment at her high school graduation and the first time she ever brought a girl home to meet her parents as a sophomore in college.

Kate enjoyed hearing the story, not only because it was DeMarco's way of opening up but because it reminded her of Melissa's childhood, how they had struggled during the pre-teen years, come close to a best friends kind of relationship, which then again became strained and distant as high school kicked in and Kate's career started to take control of her life.

When DeMarco was done, they took a moment to let the day dwindle away around them in silence. Kate watched the patrons come and go. There weren't many, as she assumed there were other more appropriate water holes elsewhere in town. But even the people who came into the seedy little motel bar looked lost and out of place. Not that they did not belong in Deton, but that their lives were stuck in some sort of limbo.

"This town," she said. "I've seen dozens of similar ones. The people are close and everyone knows one another but there are secrets. Sometimes I don't think the residents even realize they're keeping secrets. It's just…part of the lifestyle. Shit happens, you handle it, you move on. That sort of thing. It creates a very distant sort of feeling between just about everyone in town."

DeMarco slid her now-empty beer glass to the side of the table. "I can sense it, too. Even with Barnes. But I won't lie…it's not a very cheery outlook."

Kate knew it wasn't. And she hated to think in such stereotypical ways. But sometimes, in her estimation, proven history turned stereotypes into solid facts. And based on her history with places like Deton, she couldn't help but feel that whether it was intentional or not, she and DeMarco were not getting the entire story.

***

It had been a while since Kate had dreamed of Michael. The last one she'd had was more of a memory than anything else—a

48

memory of how he had nearly cut his fingers off while trying to repair the very first lawn mower they had owned, six months into their marriage.

But the one she had several hours after leaving the bar with DeMarco was nothing of that sort. In this dream, she was standing in the tiny interrogation room in the Deton PD. Michael was sitting on the other side of the little desk, looking up to her expectantly.

"You know, Michelle looks like you," he told her. "Poor Melissa…that kid got her looks from me. But our granddaughter…she looks just like you."

"I know," Kate said. "I wish you could meet her."

"Same here," he said. "But dead is dead. It's not so bad, though. If our parents were right in all that stuff they believed, I *will* get to see her one day."

"Why are you in Deton?" she asked him.

"Because you are. I'm never too far away from where you are, you know?"

"You can't be here…while I'm working. My job created too much stress between us."

"It did. But the determination in it was sexy."

He smiled and stood up from the table. It was the first time she had seen the bullet hole in the back of his head—the very bullet hole that had resulted in his death. It was not gory or gruesome; it was just there, part of him.

"Kate, is this really where you want to be?" he asked.

"Deton?"

"No…back at work. You're a grandmother now. Aren't you over all of this?"

He took her hands. They were cold and clammy. As she looked into his eyes, she saw only the whites.

"Michael…"

"Aren't you done with all of this yet?"

"I can't…"

And then he started squeezing her hands, pulling her to him so that she could feel the coldness of him, smell the graveyard stench of him.

That was when she screamed and pulled herself out of the nightmare.

She opened her eyes and stared at the ceiling, feeling the vibrations of the scream in her throat, the sound of it echoing slightly in the small motel room.

Is this really where you want to be?
Aren't you done with this yet?

They were fair questions—questions she had asked herself multiple times since coming back to the bureau. But she knew the answer to both questions...and she was fairly certain Michael would understand if he was still here.

Yes, she felt like she was supposed to be back. Even from that first call nearly a year ago, she had not felt out of touch or uncomfortable. It had been like slipping on an old glove and finding that it still fit perfectly.

She looked to the bedside clock and saw that it was 4:12 in the morning. She was pretty sure she would not be able to go back to sleep but she stayed in bed anyway. She thought of Allen and how understanding he was being in regards to her work. She thought of Melissa and Michelle, hoping that they saw her return to work as a hopeful indicator that age meant nothing and that the woman they both looked up to was strong enough for all of them.

She spent the next hour and a half in a fitful nap, dozing off for ten minutes or so and then snapping awake, over and over again.

It came to a stop when her phone started to ring. She sat up, feeling surprisingly rested, and saw an unfamiliar number on her display screen. She was pretty sure the area code was Deton.

"Hello?" she answered.

"Agent Wise, this is Officer Mark Foster. We've got movement on the case."

"What is it?" Kate asked, instantly sliding out of bed.

"Someone used Mercy Fuller's credit card late last night."

Her thought of *why does a fifteen-year-old girl have a credit card* was overruled by the jarring excitement of a potentially huge jump in the case.

"Nearby?" she asked.

"It was used at a gas station between Deton and Deerfield. And it gets even better. Security cameras at the gas station give us a clear shot of the man that used it. The time on the video footage and the time of the transaction match up perfectly."

"How long ago was the match made?"

"I got confirmation about three minutes before I called you. I looked over the video feed myself about half an hour ago. And here's the good thing about a small town...the face was familiar. All faces are familiar."

"So you know who it is?"

"I do. I double-checked in the files here at the station just to make sure, and it's a positive ID."

"Damn, Foster. Do you ever sleep?"

"Hardly," he said. And it didn't sound like he was joking. "Can you and DeMarco meet the sheriff and I at the station? I'm headed over right now."

She agreed to meet at the station as quickly as they could. She wasted no time dressing, leaving her room in her gym shorts and T-shirt right away and walking outside. She walked to the next door along the open-air corridor and started knocking. She couldn't help but smile as she knocked, waking her partner up before six in the morning. Surely, it was a good indicator that the case was moving along. And also, given her comfort level of waking DeMarco by pounding on her door in her pajamas, it was an equally good indicator that she had found a partner she trusted in DeMarco.

DeMarco answered the door, already fully alert. Kate saw that DeMarco slept in much less than she did, leaving little to the imagination. She looked away for a moment, finding the line between being professional and considerate.

"Something happen?" she asked.

"Yeah. We need to meet Barnes and Foster at the station as soon as we can."

"Give me three minutes."

And with that, they were on the move, Kate rushing back to her room with a surge of pure adrenaline propelling her forward.

CHAPTER ELEVEN

Kate drove close behind Barnes, headed down yet another back road off of Highway 44, as the first light of morning came glowing in between the trees. The residence they were headed to technically had a Deton address but was closer to Deerfield. Out on the back roads, it all looked the same to Kate and it amazed her how Barnes and Foster could differentiate each road and property.

Foster was riding shotgun with Barnes, keeping Kate informed in real-time via text. The last message he had sent told her that they were four minutes away from the suspect's home—a man named Todd Ramsey. He also informed her that they had one other unit on standby if things should get hairy. They were electing to keep the caravan to Ramsey's house small so as to not alert any news crews hiding out in the area.

They were also treating this as a high-profile crime and, as such, were prepared to go in with guns drawn. Kate didn't fully agree with this approach but it was not worth arguing over. The fact was this man had used the credit card of a girl who had been missing for three days, and all signs did indeed point to Todd Ramsey being guilty as hell.

Barnes started to slow down as they approached a house on the right side of the road. He turned quickly onto a thin strip of dirt that looked to have once been covered in gravel. The driveway was short, the house sitting less than fifty feet off of the road. Kate parked directly behind Barnes, nearly nose-to-tail. The four of them got out of their cars right away, Barnes and Foster drawing their sidearms. Kate and DeMarco stayed a few steps behind, not yet pulling their weapons. The play here was that someone local might actually recognize Barnes or Foster (and if they didn't, they'd certainly recognize the badges on their unmistakable uniforms). It might be a little more alarming and confrontational if two strange women came knocking on his door at six in the morning, aiming guns at him.

Barnes wasted no time psyching himself up or preparing. He walked directly up to the front door and knocked. He knocked hard, putting his full weight into it. The door trembled in its frame.

"Todd Ramsey! Answer the door! It's Sheriff Barnes with the Deton PD."

When there was no answer within two seconds, he repeated it all. He hammered on the door with his meaty fist and gave the same command. Only this time, he ended it with: "You have three seconds to come to the door or I *will* break it down!"

Kate heard someone yelling a response from inside, but she could not understand what was being said. She also heard running footsteps coming toward the door. Barnes stepped back, Foster flanking to his right. Kate and DeMarco stood behind them, hands on their weapons, ready to draw if necessary.

The door was opened quickly, making all four of them tense up. But when Kate saw the absolute terror and confusion on the face of the man that stood there, she stood down a bit. He was dressed only in boxers, still pulling on a pair of pants as he stood at the door. Todd Ramsey's hair was tousled and in disarray. His eyes were till slightly hazed from sleep. He looked to be about forty-five or so—and many of those years had been hard ones. He noticed that Barnes had his gun drawn and took a clumsy step back.

"What's going on?" Todd Ramsey asked. He sounded like he was on the verge of tears.

Barnes did not ask to be invited inside. He simply walked through the opened front door with Foster on his heels. Barnes turned back to Kate and gave her a nod, indicating that he wanted her to pick it up from here.

He's smart, she thought. *He used local credentials to get things started and now that we're inside, it becomes more legitimate.*

"Mr. Ramsey, we have proof that you paid for gasoline last night with a credit card that is not yours. Would you like to tell us where you got the card?"

He looked instantly guilty, but the confusion was still on his face. "Yeah...shit, sorry. But is that what this is about? That card..."

"That credit card belonged to a fifteen-year-old girl named Mercy Fuller," Kate said, putting on her best authoritative voice. It was pleasing to see just how easily she could still slip in and out of it.

"That name ring a bell?" Barnes said.

"No, it—"

"I find that hard to believe," Kate interrupted. "Her name has been all over the news. A local girl. Think hard."

"That's right," he said, his voice trembling. "Her folks were killed. But I had no idea it was her card."

"Mr. Ramsey, this is quite serious," Kate said. "Mercy Fuller has been missing for three days now. And all of a sudden, you're found using her credit card."

The weight of what they were accusing him of seemed to land on him like a bomb. His eyes grew wide and he took another step backward. "Whoa. Hold on. No."

"No what?" Foster asked.

"I have nothing to do with it! I swear, I had no idea it was her card!"

"Where is it that card now?" Kate asked.

"In my wallet."

"Where?" Barnes asked.

"In my bedroom, on my dresser."

"You stay here, Mr. Ramsey. I'll go have a look. Any wife or kids back there I need to know about?"

"No. I'm divorced. I—"

"Where's the bedroom?"

"Last door on the left. But I—"

But Barnes was already gone, walking quickly out of the living room and down the hallway that branched off of it.

"This is messed up," Todd said. "I had no idea…"

"Where did you find the card, Mr. Ramsey?" DeMarco asked.

"Out in the woods, right on the side of a little dirt road." He looked to Foster and added: "It's the one the local kids call Blood Gulch. You know it?"

"I know it. Why were you out there anyway?"

"Just driving. I do it sometimes, you know. Just to clear my head. I got out of the truck to take a piss and saw it."

"And when you saw the name on it—the name Mercy Fuller— you didn't make the connection to the news story?" Kate asked.

"No. There's no way I would have. That's not the name on it. The name Fuller *is* on it, but the first name is just an initial and it's not M."

"I need you to sit down slowly on your couch," Kate said. "Hands stay on your knees. We're going to have a look around your house and your property for any traces of Mercy Fuller."

"That's insane! I have no idea what happened to her!"

"Then you won't mind us looking, now will you?"

As Todd sat down slowly on his couch, Barnes came back from the bedroom. He had the credit card in his hand, showing it to Kate and DeMarco. "The card is made out to W. Fuller. I'm assuming that's Wendy Fuller."

"Then why would it show up as Mercy Fuller?" Foster asked.

"A lot of parents sign off on credit cards for their kids," DeMarco said. "My own folks did it with me. A way to test responsibility and all of that."

"Is that common around here?" Kate asked.

"No idea," Barnes said. "Why any fifteen-year-old needs a credit card is beyond me. But that brings us back to you, Mr. Ramsey. Where did you find this if not plucking it right off of Mercy Fuller?"

"I already told them! I found in out on Blood Gulch Road. Right there on the side."

"Now that seems like a stretch of good luck, doesn't it? And even if that's the truth, did you not think to turn it in? You figure it was yours if you found it? Finders keepers?"

"I'm not proud of it, okay? I felt bad but...hell, I can barely make my bills now. I got laid off two weeks ago and can't find work. It's been tough. One lousy tank of gas for my truck. That's all I got with it."

"Nice sob story," Barnes said. "Officer Foster, would you stay here with Mr. Ramsey while I check the place over with Agents Wise and DeMarco?"

Foster gave a no-nonsense nod and sat down in a small recliner that was adjacent to the couch. Barnes gave Ramsey another distrustful glance before he headed for the door. Kate and DeMarco stepped out with him, walking back out into the early morning. They walked to the east side of the house, the large backyard giving way to the forests beyond.

If Todd Ramsey was indeed keeping Mercy Fuller, Kate saw no immediate areas he could be hiding her. There were no sheds, no garage, no barn, no suspicious trailers or other structures on the property.

"You know this guy at all?" DeMarco asked Barnes.

"Not well, no. Hardly at all, really. Just in a passing sort of way."

"So you have no real reason to suspect that he would take Mercy?"

"Other than the fact that he has her credit card, you mean?"

Kate nodded, understanding that Barnes was starting to take the case rather personally. He just wanted it wrapped so the people in his town could sleep easier—so the news crews would finally just get the hell out of his town.

With that in mind, Kate dutifully assisted as they looked around Ramsey's property. They checked the tree line around the forest, they scouted his house, looked through the basement and even, after much debate and arguing with Ramsey, looked at his car and old pickup truck. The entire process took about half an hour. Kate knew within about ten minutes that Mercy Fuller was nowhere on Todd Ramsey's property. It just didn't add up; it didn't make sense.

Ramsey's car was the last place they checked. Barnes closed the trunk and leaned against the back of the car. The look he gave the agents was a helpless one—a man asking for help without using any words.

"So what do we do now?" he asked.

"We have Mr. Ramsey take us out to this Blood Gulch Road," Kate said. "Make him show us where he found the credit card."

Even as she said it, Kate could feel that it was a thin lead at best. But the fact remained that they now had in their possession something that likely was on Mercy Fuller's person on the day she went missing—discovered randomly by Todd Ramsey. Weak lead or not, she felt that they were at least still moving forward.

And as long as they had momentum on their side, Kate knew there was hope.

CHAPTER TWELVE

Even with Officer Foster leaving to return to the station, the car felt incredibly crowded with Todd Ramsey sitting in the back beside DeMarco. It wasn't just that there were four people crammed into Barnes' patrol car—Kate and Barnes up front, DeMarco and Ramsey in the back—it was also the added fear, tension, and confusion coming off of Ramsey. No more than three minutes after they had left Ramsey's house, it was just too much for Kate. She knew from experience that silence in tense situations never led to anything good. So she did her best to defuse it before it was too late.

"Mr. Ramsey, why were you out driving so late at night anyway?"

"Like I said. I was just clearing my head. I've always liked to drive around the back roads at night—especially those old dirt and gravel roads no one really ever uses. It's been a rough few weeks and I was just getting antsy sitting around the house."

"What did you do for a living?"

"I was a tree-topper for a local lumber company. I got laid off when the lumber yards cut back the quotas. I knew it was coming…it's been happening to other companies all year. Some say because of the government shutdown. I don't know…"

And just like that, Kate knew she had succeeded. She had not related to him per se, but she had him speaking to her about something other than the disappearance and the murders of the Fuller family. Ramsey seemed to be at ease, still clearly unhappy to be in the back of a police car but not quite as tense.

Fifteen minutes after leaving Ramsey's house, Barnes turned onto yet another back road. This one wound like a snake even deeper into the forest. Kate saw a few small houses tucked back in coves of trees, a good distance off of the road. These were houses that were clearly being lived in but were about two or three paychecks away from squalor. There were weeded yards, collapsed porches, wandering pet dogs in desperate need of a meal. Just as Kate had started to understand the state of this part of the county, Barnes turned onto a road that started out with a sign that read: End State Maintenance 0.5 Miles.

"Blood Gulch Road sees a lot of traffic during hunting season," Barnes explained. "There are all of these little turn-offs into big open fields or off-roading-type roads that used to be logging roads."

"Deer or turkey hunting?" DeMarco asked.

"Both. It's one of the reasons locals have dubbed it Blood Gulch Road."

"One of the reasons?" Kate asked.

"Yeah. I guarantee you we catch at least twenty or so cars every year out here at night…kids coming to have sex. It sort of got that reputation…a place where local girls came to offer up their virginity and…"

"I got you," Kate said. "No further explanation needed."

They came to the spot where state maintenance came to an end, the rough tar surface giving way to a dirt road. The sun was nearly at full blast as 7:30 in the morning approached, painting a muddy golden hue over the road.

"The spot is about another mile ahead," Ramsey said. "Just before you get to the Jones Field. You know that little side road?"

"I know it," Barnes said, aggravated.

They drove on, the cruiser kicking up little plumes of dust behind them. The car remained in silence again until, about two minutes later, Ramsey sat forward in his seat. "It's right there," he said. "That's where I pulled over."

Barnes pulled the car over to the side of the road and wasted no time getting out. All four of them piled out of the car and stood along the edge of the road. "Where was the card?" Barnes asked.

Ramsey walked to the back of the car and looked in all directions. He seemed to be giving it some serious thought, wanting to be absolutely sure. After a few seconds, he pointed to a spot just ahead of the car, to the left. He walked over to it, took two steps off of the road and into the overgrown grass along the side, and nodded.

"Right there," he said. "I saw it so easily because it wasn't lying down flat. It had gotten caught up in some of the weeds and was sort of standing a bit."

Kate took a step back, wanting to be able to take in the entirety of the scene. She saw no blood, no clear indications that anything bad had happened in this spot. She could also see no clear traces that anyone had passed through the area on foot. Beyond the overgrowth of grass on the side of the road, there were only trees and shadows.

"Sheriff, what's on the other side of those trees?" Kate asked.

He thought about it for a while, perhaps checking out a map of the area in his head. "This little strip of forest goes on for a few miles. Two, maybe three. And then it empties out at Jones Field...just a big old strip of undeveloped land that becomes popular during hunting season."

"That's a lot of ground to cover," DeMarco commented.

"Well," Kate said, "with the discovery of the credit card at this very spot and the fact that she's now been missing for three days, I can contact some folks at the state PD. Get some manpower and some bloodhounds. If we need it, I can maybe get a few more bureau eyes down here as well."

"I can get on that right now," Barnes said. "I figure the dogs could be down here within a few hours."

"Make the call," Kate said. "In the meantime, I'll see what I can do to get the bureau to put some push behind it. If we—"

Her phone rang, buzzing from her pocket and interrupting her. She answered it, still looking out into the forest and imagining all of the possibilities out there.

"This is Agent Wise," she said into the phone.

"Agent Wise, this is Jan Pettus...Anne's mother. Do you have a moment?"

"Of course. What can I do for you?"

"I thought you might want to know that Anne woke up this morning and came to me right away. She said she just remembered something she forgot to tell you when you were asking about Mercy having any jobs."

"Is she available to speak with me?" Kate asked.

"Not right now. She's getting ready to finally go back to school. But she told me what she remembered. And honestly...I even knew about it but didn't think anything of it." She paused here, almost as if for dramatic effect. "Earlier this year, she babysat for a local couple that was going through a hard time. Maybe just two or three times, Anne says, though she's not absolutely certain."

"Does she remember anything in particular about this family?"

"Well, everyone in town knows that they were going through a hard time. No one knows quite why, though. Rumor has it that the husband was cheating on his wife and they spent a lot of time apart...so the kids sometimes got caught in the middle. They were friends with the Fullers and apparently, Mercy stepped in as babysitter."

"What's the family name?"

She saw that Barnes was listening in now, his interest piqued as he stood by the side of the car, keeping a distrustful eye on Todd

Ramsey. She listened as Mrs. Pettus told her what she knew, which wasn't much: a name and a general location of where the father—now divorced—was living.

The call was over ten seconds later. She pocketed her phone and looked back to the strip of grass beside the road. She wondered how the credit card had gotten there. Had it been discarded as someone had pulled Mercy Fuller into the woods or had her abductor (assuming there was one) thrown it out in an attempt to get rid of any evidence?

"Sheriff? What can you tell me about a man named Edgar Lee?" she asked.

"A Deton native. Went through a nasty divorce end of last year, or early this year. His wife and kids moved somewhere further south. He stayed here, keeps working on a farm that should have given up the ghost about ten years ago. In my estimated opinion, the guy is sort of a sleazeball." He raised an eyebrow and tilted his head. "Why do you ask?"

"Because I believe Agent DeMarco and I are going to pay him a visit."

CHAPTER THIRTEEN

Barnes knew exactly where the farm was and gave them directions easily. While he returned to the station to get the state police further involved with the investigation into Mercy Fuller's disappearance, Kate and DeMarco headed out toward what Barnes had referred to as the Lee Farm. Along the way, DeMarco called both the bureau and the state police to request any records on Edgar Lee. When she got off of the phone with the bureau, she had quite a bit to share.

"I think I may have just found out one of the reasons for the Lees' divorce," DeMarco said. "Three years ago, Edgar Lee was arrested for attempting to download illegal pornography."

"Children?" Kate asked, horrified.

"No. But just as bad. Some sixteen-year-old that was selling videos online. He got off on a technicality, as he never *actually* downloaded it. But when an investigation was conducted, they did find questionable content on his computer. Girls that, while there were obviously no ages given, certainly did not look to be eighteen."

"Any word on how old his kids were when all of that went down?"

"No. But state PD did confirm the divorce was finalized last year. The wife has a restraining order filed against him. They say other than the severe porn mark on file, there's no other record on the guy."

This information weighed heavily on them as they approached Lee farm. It sat just slightly outside of the Deton town limits, tucked away down a driveway that was at least a quarter of a mile long. Once the driveway ended and the surrounding forests opened up, it revealed a rustic-looking barn. It was quaint and beautiful in a derelict kind of way—the sort of thing one might see in paintings on a dentist's office or in calendars depicting whimsical scenes.

Kate parked the car at the end of the driveway, behind a large pickup truck with Farm Use tags. They stepped out of the car and walked into the large front yard. The house was a two-story farmhouse; while it was in need of many repairs, it was still a fairly beautiful house. Because the farm was named after a family, Kate wondered how long the house had been standing here.

As they neared the house, they hard a series of thumps and thuds coming from behind the house, accompanied a male voice uttering a few quiet curses. Exchanging a look of caution, they walked around the side of the house and more of the property came into view. A single large barn sat roughly fifty yards away from the house. A few other sheds sat beside it and off to the distance. Beyond that were what looked like emaciated corn fields and large fields of varying crops that Kate could not tell the difference between.

The commotion was coming from the larger barn. As they approached it, Kate noticed the faint wailing of an '80s country song, something by Randy Travis, coming from the barn. The doors were open, revealing a huge open space. On one side, there were a few chicken coops, all vacant. On the other side was various farming equipment lined up almost methodically: a tractor, bailing wire, a stack of old two-by-fours, shelves of seeds and fertilizer, and sacks full of hay and grain.

Two men were standing by the two-by-fours, making another stack with several other boards strewn at their feet. Before entering the barn, Kate knocked as loudly as she could on the massive open door. Both men turned to look at them. Neither of them were wearing shirts. One of the men looked to be about twenty or so, his chest and stomach chiseled and his shoulders bulky. The other man was middle-aged, his hair starting to go gray.

"Can I help you?" the older man asked.

"Is one of you gentlemen Edgar Lee?"

"That's me," the older man said. "Who's asking?"

Showing her ID, Kate stepped inside, DeMarco behind her. "We're Agents Wise and DeMarco with the FBI. We were hoping to ask you a few questions."

The baffled look on his face was nearly comical. He swiped sweat from his brow with a bandana and collected his shirt from a nearby post. "Can I ask what about?"

"Of course. But perhaps not in front of present company," she said, nodding toward the younger man.

Lee slipped his shirt on and walked over to the agents. "FBI?" he asked. "Seriously? I think there might be some kind of mistake." He then lowered his voice and said: "Is it about the same things from three years ago?"

"Not exactly," Kate said. They were outside of the barn now, walking together through the yard in the direction of the house. "I assume that being from Deton, you heard about what happened to the Fullers."

"I did. God, that was terrible. From what I hear, the theory is that Mercy killed them and then left town."

"We're not here to discuss theories," DeMarco said. "We're trying to find out exactly what happened and we discovered that Mercy served as a babysitter for you when the divorce started to go nasty."

"Well, hell...you two just go right for the heart, huh?"

"A girl is missing and her parents are dead," Kate said. "So yes...please forgive us if we don't waste any time getting to the point."

"So are you here to ask about the working relationship when she was babysitting? Or are you here to remind me that I made some very stupid mistakes three years ago?"

"A bit of both," Kate said. "I'd first like to know how the hell you were able to get the Fullers to allow their daughter to babysit for you with the questionable pornography charges on your record."

"I was never convicted," he said. "There's nothing that happened that labeled me as a sex offender or any nonsense like that. And Lydia, my ex-wife, was generous enough to keep the secret. No sense in ruining my reputation and all that. It's the one nice thing she did during that last year of marriage."

"So the Fullers had no idea? We understand that you and your wife were once friends with the Fullers."

"We were. But when the marriage fell apart, a lot of people in town chose to take sides. And the Fullers chose my wife. It's one of the reasons they asked Mercy to stop babysitting for me."

They stopped near the backyard. Apparently, Edgar Lee had no intention of inviting them into his home.

"What *was* that working relationship like?" Kate asked.

"There wasn't much of one at all. She'd come watch the kids while I was out dealing with lawyers or just taking some time to blow off steam. I'd see her for about five minutes when she arrived and then her parents would come get her when I got home."

"Did she call her parents when you arrived back home, asking them to come pick her up?"

"Yes."

"So how long would you say she was typically in your house between the time she called her parents to the time they actually showed up?"

"I don't know," he said, clearly irritated. "And quite frankly, I don't like what you're implying."

"I don't expect you to," Kate said. "But based on what we know of you—the charges of potentially underage pornography and an affair, for instance—we have to work with what we have. So, if you could tell us as much about the time you spent with Mercy Fuller, it would be greatly appreciated."

"I just did. When I came in, I usually went right to the fridge and grabbed a beer. She only babysat for me three times. Each time, she sat in the living room and watched TV while I drank a beer in the kitchen. I'm not stupid…I knew my history would piss people off if they knew about it. I kept my distance and spoke to her as little as possible."

"Who else knew about this babysitting job?"

"My wife, her parents, apparently whoever told you. We tried to keep it quiet because of my history but this fucking town…no one can keep a secret."

"Mr. Lee, would you mind if we had a look around the premises?" DeMarco asked.

"For what, exactly?"

"To rule you out as a suspect."

"You see me as a suspect?" he barked.

"A man on the edge of a divorce, having an affair, with a history of interest in teen pornography…yes. I'd say you're a suspect at this point."

Kate hoped DeMarco would quiet down but could tell that she was only getting ramped up. She was quickly learning that issues of child endangerment were a hot button for DeMarco. She was speaking to Lee in a condescending tone, as if trying to goad him.

Apparently, it worked.

When he stepped forward and raised his hand to punch DeMarco, it took them both by surprise. Kate, standing to the right, acted on pure instinct. While DeMarco saw the punch coming and went into a defensive posture, Kate caught Lee's arm, twisted it down and back at the same time, and then swept his legs out from under him.

He hit the ground with a thump, all of the air rocketing out of him.

"That was unnecessary," Kate said as she brought out her handcuffs. The remark was directed at Lee but she hoped DeMarco had caught her gist as well.

"You can't do this," Lee hissed. "I've done nothing wrong!"

"Had you not taken a swing at an FBI agent, you'd be right," Kate said. "We'd ask a few more questions and then be on our way." She slapped the cuffs on him and then, with DeMarco's help, got him to his feet. "But now you'll be spending some time at the Deton PD, answering even more questions."

Lee struggled against them for a moment but then seemed to think better of it. As Kate led him back to the car, she looked back behind them. She saw the sheds behind the barn, all rather old and in bad shape.

Any of them would be the perfect place to hide someone... or a body, she thought.

Her eyes remained on the sheds even as she and DeMarco escorted Edgar Lee into the back of their car.

***

Within ten minutes of making the call, both Barnes and Foster showed up at Lee Farm. While the local police stood guard over Edgar Lee and asked him questions, Kate and DeMarco investigated Lee's property.

The barn was obviously the epicenter of the day-to-day farm operations. The only questionable things found inside the barn were a few porno magazines hidden in the bottom of a toolbox and an old laptop. The laptop, while clearly quite old, was of particular interest because even though it seemed to have been discarded under a few receipts and empty nail boxes on a workbench, it still had a charge of about thirty percent—indicating that it had been used recently. When Kate turned it on, it came to a password screen, making it impossible for her to see what was on it.

The sheds came next. One looked to have been disregarded a long time ago, still standing only out of some family obligation. It was empty with the exception of several dried wasp nests in the rafters and junked parts to what looked to be a very old tractor. The other two held only old farming equipment; one of the sheds was packed with the stuff: ancient tires, old rakes and hoes, a bail of copper wire. A small shelf sat on the far wall, stacked with a few farming magazines. A small drugstore calendar sat there as well, offering a month-by-month depiction of 1989.

With the investigation over, Kate and DeMarco walked back to the driveway. Lee was in the back of Barnes' car while Barnes and Foster spoke to him through the opened back window. Kate brought the old laptop with her, not wanting to run the risk of leaving it behind if it did have something of interest on it. The fact that it was old, partially charged, and hanging out in his barn seemed somewhat peculiar as far as she was concerned.

"Anything?" Barnes asked.

"Other than taking a swing at an agent, not so much," Kate said. "I think it might be worth looking into what might be on this laptop, though. Got anyone at the station that can get into it?"

"Sadly, no."

"I can take a crack at it," DeMarco said. "I was kind of a tech geek in high school and college—something I still tinker with."

"You get anything else out of him?" Kate asked.

"Just the woe is me, everyone-is-out-to-get-me diatribe."

Kate noticed that Lee was very tense as he sat in the back of the patrol car. His eyes were locked on the laptop in her hands, making her think it was a good idea to bring it after all.

"Want to huddle up at the station, then?" Barnes asked. "Staties are on their way…should be here in about an hour or so. Canine unit will be pretty much right behind them."

"We'll meet you there," Kate said, wasting no time and getting into her car. She was starting to think there might indeed be something on the laptop. Maybe not anything directly related to Mercy Fuller, but certainly something that would shed more light onto Edgar Lee and if he was hiding anything from them.

"Hey, Kate?" DeMarco said as they made their way back up the driveway. "I feel like I maybe owe you an apology."

"For what?"

"For losing it on Lee…for just laying into him. Honestly, I was hoping he'd snap…hoping he'd try something. Men that get their thrills on young girls get under my skin in a way that I'm not particularly proud of."

"I get it," she said. "I've done the same thing in the past. Goading people you think are guilty into doing or saying something stupid used to be my weapon of choice. But I think if I hadn't have stopped that punch, you might have a busted nose right now."

"Yeah, you handled that like a beast. Are you okay?"

"I'm fine." It wasn't totally the truth. Her right shin was flaring with little spark of pain from where she had swept Lee to the ground. While she was still fit, she was not conditioned to that sort of physical altercation. She was not looking forward to the soreness and the bruising that was going to come as a result.

They got back out on the road and followed Barnes and Foster back to the police station. Kate once again found herself drawn to the way the trees seemed to almost lean in toward them. It made her feel like the forest was keeping some deep, dark secret and it would do anything it could to keep it hidden.

CHAPTER FOURTEEN

All charges against Jeremy Branch in the Mercy Fuller case were dropped the night before around nine o'clock. He was still in a heap of trouble due to the drug possession and possible rape charges from other footage found on his phone. So when Barnes and Foster escorted Edgar Lee into the Deton PD, the interrogation room was available. Kate and DeMarco followed close behind him. Kate took note of the two news vans in the parking lot, the news anchors and camera people scrambling to catch up to them before they made it inside.

When they entered, there were phones ringing and officers talking over one another. Kate caught a flustered look on Barnes' face as they led Lee to the interrogation room. "You okay, Sheriff?" she asked.

"Yeah. It's just that this case is making me realize just how small-time we are. One interrogation room…less than ten officers on staff. When the state guys show up, this place is going to be packed out."

"Well, let's see how much we can get done before they show up, what do you say?"

"If you can handle interrogation," DeMarco said to Kate, "I can get started on trying to get into the laptop."

"That's perfect."

"Foster, why don't you go with Agent DeMarco? Anything she needs, you do your damndest to get it for her."

With their assignments in order, Kate and Barnes entered the tiny interrogation room with Lee. He sat down on the other side of the desk rigidly, as if he might started fighting at any moment. But the moment his butt was in the seat, he seemed to switch gears, kicking into apologetic mode.

"Look," he said. "I lost my temper and took a swing at your partner. But she was pushing. She was bringing up things from my past that I have tried very hard to put behind me." He sighed heavily and then added: "If you'll bring her in here, I'll apologize."

"I'm sure she'd appreciate that," Kate said. "First, since you seem to be in a bargaining mood, I need you to tell me everything there is to know about the time you spent with Mercy Fuller."

"I'm not proud of it...but I *made* myself not speak to her. I *had* to be in another room. I didn't trust myself with her. I know...I know some of the things I've been in trouble for in the past are messed up. I knew it then...when she was at my house, waiting for her father to pick her up. I swear to you...I never so much as touched her."

It was the trembling in his jaw and the way he kneaded his hands together that made Kate believe him. Still, he remained tense and nervous. He was hiding *something*.

"Did you interact with Mercy at all when you and your ex-wife were friends with the Fullers?" Kate asked.

"Nothing beyond waving hello or asking if she wanted a snack or a drink on the few times they came over. She was pretty good friends with my oldest daughter. Whenever our families were together, the two of them would hang out most of the time."

"And where is your family living right now?"

"Somewhere near the North Carolina border. A small town— even smaller than Deton, I think—in the middle of nowhere."

Kate figured if it came to it, they could get contact information for his ex-wife and children. But she was pretty sure that would not be necessary. She still had one weapon in her arsenal, one more mode of attack that might give them everything they needed.

"My partner is currently trying to crack into the old laptop we found in the barn. I find it suspicious that an older model laptop—at least seven or eight years old—was in your barn, partially charged."

"Why? Laptops are expensive. I've had that one for years. It runs slow, but does the job. Why get a new one? I work on a farm. A laptop isn't necessarily a necessity."

"I'd agree with that," Kate said, trying to disarm him. "What do you use it for?"

"Music. Some YouTube stuff. Old wrestling videos, mainly. I use iTunes sometimes, too. But it lags sometimes." He chuckled nervously here and said: "So maybe it *is* time for me to try to get a new one, huh?"

"Would you give us the password to get into it, then?"

Lee paused for a moment, still wringing his hands as he considered the question. Slowly, he started to shake his head. "No. I'm not going to do that. That's an invasion of privacy."

"Right now, you are in custody for attacking an agent," Kate said. "But given the nature of your history and your relationship with Mercy Fuller, we can stretch that to holding you as a suspect in her disappearance. That would give us every lawful right to do whatever we need to your laptop. With some paperwork, we could

68

also have a look around your house and the entire farm. So why not save us the time and tell us the password for your laptop?"

Again, he shook his head. But the taut expression on his face indicated that he knew he was essentially screwed.

"Don't be an idiot," Barnes said, stepping forward. "If Agent DeMarco can't crack it, someone with the state PD will. And I've got state units on the way to help in the search for Mercy Fuller right now. One way or the other, we're going to find out what's on there. And the longer you refuse to give us a password, the more certain we become that you're hiding something."

Lee said nothing. He slowly sat back in the chair, trying to get more comfortable.

"Do you think you're proving something?" Barnes asked. "Buying yourself more time, maybe? You—"

"Sheriff, can I speak with you outside?" Kate asked.

Barnes nodded, making a little chuffing noise in the general direction of Lee. Kate opened the door to the interrogation room, letting Barnes go out ahead of her. They took a few steps away from the closed interrogation room door before Kate said anything.

"He's guilty of *something,* but I'm becoming more and more sure it has nothing to do with Mercy Fuller."

"Any ideas?" Barnes asked.

"Based on studies and past cases I've heard about, there seems to be significant evidence that men that are addicted to pornography rarely ever truly get over it. And if Edgar Lee's preferences of the past teach us anything...well, let's just say I'm not going to be surprised if we find a lot of underage pornography on this laptop."

Barnes nodded, his hands on his hips. He managed to crack a dry smile when he said, "Well, if nothing else, we've discovered where a lot of Deton's drugs are coming from and we've potentially busted a man for child pornography...all while trying to crack the Fuller case. So then why does it feel like we're still losing?"

"Because there's still a girl out there somewhere, and we need to find her."

"Do you think she's still alive?" He asked the question quietly, like he really wasn't sure if he wanted an answer.

"I don't know," she answered honestly. "But I do know that every minute that passes without us finding her, her chances become that much smaller."

Again, all Barnes could do was nod. He hunched his shoulders and walked toward his office, taking the weight of not only the case but the entire town with him.

CHAPTER FIFTEEN

Mercy would never admit it to any of her friends—especially not Anne—but she was a closet Taylor Swift fan. Mercy had even liked her at the start of the singer's career, when she'd been a country act. The only person who knew Mercy was a Taylor Swift fan was her mother...and that was only because she had walked into Mercy's room when Mercy had been jamming out to "Blank Space" a year or so ago. It was a memory that Mercy held dear because rather than teasing her, her mother had danced with her in a spontaneous moment of goofiness—a moment that had ended with her mother making a shushing gesture and saying: *"Your secret is safe with me."*

Mercy thought about that moment as she once again traced the shape and size of her dark prison. She thought of her mother, trying to grasp the fact that both of her parents were now dead. Or so she assumed, anyway. The way her father had screamed for her to run...there had been terror in his voice. And then the gunshots...

Thankfully, Mercy had "Blank Space" on repeat in her head, drowning out the sound of that memory.

She came to the end of what she was starting to think of as her prison cell. She felt the corner, where the two walls met. She was fairly certain that was she was thinking of as "the end" of her cell was a door of some kind. Based on the size and shape of whatever she was being held in, she thought the door would be the kind that rolled up, like the back of a U-Haul. When she thought of that, she was pretty sure the shape and size of her prison was pretty close to that. Maybe she was in a storage unit, or one of those big moving containers.

She got down on her hands and knees and felt at the space where the floor met what she now assumed was a door. There was the slightest dip between the floor and all five feet of the door. In the center of it, she felt some sort of indentation in the door—one that was supposed to be there, perhaps feeding further down into the floor where some kind of a latch held the door closed. She dug her fingers into that indentation but could feel nothing. If she was being held in some sort of moving container or trailer, she was pretty sure the only way to open it was from the outside.

As she investigated the door, she heard a light squeaking noise coming from somewhere off in the distance. It sounded like a door opening and then closing. She then heard light footsteps and then…whistling.

It was him. He was back.

He had come to her three times. So far, he had not actually come into her little prison. He had only come to the door to speak with her—to tease her. She supposed if he *did* ever actually come inside her prison, she would have to fight. She'd fight as much as she could because her mind went to the worst possible place: that he would rape her or kill her.

She backed away from the door. Instinct told her to go back and cower in the corner. But if he *did* come inside, that would be the worst place for her to be. He wouldn't be expecting her to be right there at the door, waiting.

She decided right then and there that if he opened the door, she was going to make a run for it. She'd go right past him and slide out one of the far sides of the door. Her knees ached in anticipation, wanting to run.

The man tapped on the door from the outside. The sound was hollow but almost musical. "How's my little one?" he asked.

She said nothing. She waited to see what else he had to say. She wondered if there was some way she could *make* him open the door. She knew she couldn't open it from the inside. So if he would just open it…then maybe she'd have a chance.

"Answer me, Mercy."

He knows my name, she thought. It sent a flare of terror through her heart. Still, she said nothing.

"Here's the deal," the man said. "I've had you for a little over three days. I know you're hungry. Those crackers aren't cutting it. And how many sodas do you have left? Wouldn't you like some refreshing cold water?"

Her mouth ached at the mention of cold water. She almost spoke out to him at the mere thought of it. It was like a chess game, trying to figure out what his next move might be.

"Let me try it this way, then," he said. "Mercy…no one knows where you are. Only me. I hold your fate in my hands. After a while, I suppose I'll let you go. Maybe. But if you stand any chance of making it back home, you are going to have to talk to me. Do you understand?" He paused here for a moment and then, with delight in his voice, he added: "Besides, you miss your parents, right? Don't you want to know how they're doing? All you have to do it speak with me a bit…and I'll let you know."

She stifled back a cry at the thought of her parents. And with that surge of emotion, she was unable to keep her words from coming out.

"What do you want?" she asked.

"Ah, there's my girl. You have a beautiful voice, Mercy."

"What do you *want*?" she asked again, her voice tearful and broken this time.

"Just to know you better. For example, what is your favorite color?"

It was such an unexpected question that she wasn't sure she had heard him correctly at first. "Purple," she said.

"Ah, yes. That's a favorite of mine, too. And what is your favorite food?"

Her stomach seemed to buckle at the thought of it, and the answer came out of her mouth right away. "Cheeseburgers."

"I'm more of a shrimp man myself," he said. His voice was overly cheerful; he was loving every moment of this.

"Do you have a boyfriend?" he asked.

She wasn't sure what to say. The truth of the matter was that she didn't. Not really. Jeremy Branch didn't count...did he? Still, she figured she should answer with what she thought he wanted to hear.

"No."

"Really? A girl as pretty as you? Well...have you ever kissed a boy?"

"Yes."

"Have you ever had sex with a boy?"

The question made her angry for reasons she did not fully understand. It was private and certainly not something she wanted to share with a man that had abducted her...a man she had never even seen.

"Where are my parents?" she asked.

"We'll get to that later, Mercy. You have my word. But you need to answer my questions first. Now tell me, Mercy. Have you had sex with a boy?"

"Yes."

"Hmm," he said. It sounded almost sensual and made Mercy feel dirty. Slowly, he started to back away from the door. The last thing she'd expected to feel in this situation was shame. And with each new question he asked her, the feeling was worse.

"Did you like it?" he asked. And before she could answer him, he kept going. "Oh, I bet you did. I bet you loved it. How did you take it?"

Mercy started to weep. She balled her fists to her eyes and slowly slid down against the wall, sinking to the floor.

"It's okay, you know?" he said. His voice was quiet, reasoning. "I had no delusions. You're beautiful. I'm sure many boys were tripping over themselves for a chance to be with you. I did not think I would be the first."

The first? she thought. *So he does plan on raping me...*

"But you know what, Mercy? I'm sure between you and I, we can find something you haven't done with a boy. I mean, there are *lots* of things we can do. I'm sure we can think of something."

Everything went quiet then. Mercy wasn't sure, but she thought she could hear him breathing heavily.

If he comes in now, I won't be able to fight him. I'm too weak, I'm too—

Something slammed hard into the side of the door outside. The reverberation coursed through her bones.

"Tell me what you can do for me that you haven't done for another boy," he said. He sounded angry now, making her assume that the loud noise had been him striking the side of the door.

"Please," she said, still crying. "Just tell me about my parents."

"You're not playing nice," he said. "It's important that we know one another first."

"Please…"

"Is that really what you want, pet?"

"Yes," she sobbed.

There was a moment's pause and then his answer. He spoke slowly and deliberately, as if savoring each word. "Your parents are dead. I killed them. Your father first and then your mother. I would be having this conversation with your delicious-looking mother but I knew you were there, too. And I had to have you."

"No…"

"Yes. I killed them both. Your mother begged me to spare you. But before the light went out of her eyes, I promised her I'd care for you. That I'd take care of you and—"

He said more, but Mercy tuned it out. She went into some ethereal void within her head where nothing existed…nothing other than the image of dancing with her mother like two goofballs to "Blank Space" by Taylor Swift.

And even beyond that, there was oblivion—a darkness beyond the darkness of her prison that she slowly and deliberately sank into as her abductor's voice droned on and on as if on some other world.

CHAPTER SIXTEEN

The state police arrived at the Deton police department at 11:05 in the morning. DeMarco had not yet managed to tap into Edgar Lee's laptop and Lee himself had not yet started talking—not even so much as asking for a lawyer. With the arrival of what Barnes kept referring to as "the Staties," the place seemed to go into a tailspin. News crews clambered for the best position, only to get a string of "no comment" from the state police, Barnes, and Kate. The bullpen at the station became a madhouse as the state police started coordinating with officers like Foster and Barnes, while also being filled in on the inner workings of the case by Kate and DeMarco.

Kate started to feel the start of a headache brewing behind her eyes as she and DeMarco sat down with Barnes and the state trooper in charge of the trio of officers that had showed up. His name was Dale Murphy, a rotund African-American man who had the look of an officer of the law who had seen way too much shit in his time.

"Canine units are already on the way to the scene you indicated to us on the phone," Murphy told Barnes. He then looked to Kate and DeMarco and added: "As for the laptop, we can't help there. That's going to probably be something that would be faster handled on your end."

"I don't even know that it matters," Kate said. "It's doubtful that whatever crimes he has hiding on that laptop is linked to the Fuller case. In terms of priorities, I'd say it's low."

"I've got a piece of software running on it right now that should be able to crack it open," DeMarco said. "But that can be running in the background."

"What else can we assist with?" Murphy asked.

"I think that covers it," Kate said. "This case has essentially become a manhunt. The hope, as far as I can see it, is that we find Mercy Fuller alive and she will know who abducted her and killed her parents."

"So it's just scouring the forests for any signs of her—dead or alive?" Murphy asked.

"Seems that way for now. With her parents dead and no next of kin in town, there aren't any further resources. Edgar Lee was our last one and, as I've said, I honestly don't think he had any hand in the disappearance."

Murphy shrugged and looked around the table. "Agents Wise and DeMarco...this is your show so long as you're here in Deton. Give us the orders and we'll jump."

"Let your canine units know we're on the way. Find out where they feel we would best be used in terms of searching the forest on foot."

Murphy gave a polite nod and headed out to do just that. Kate and DeMarco also got up, a feeling of urgency pushing them. Kate had been on five different cases over her career where the entirety of a case had all come down to an on-foot manhunt. Four of those five cases had turned up a dead body; the fifth had resulted in them just barely getting to the victim in time, ushering her on to a three-week hospital stay but, ultimately, a full life afterward. She knew the urgency of the situation and did her best to remain upbeat.

On the way toward the front door, Kate paused at the door to the interrogation room. She figured she'd leave instruction with someone to release Edgar Lee in the next hour or so. They could keep his laptop a while longer and if anything came out of it, they could simply arrest him again. For now, though, she didn't see the sense in keeping him around when the PD had already become a miniature madhouse.

She reached for the door handle as her eyes fell on DeMarco. She was sitting back behind the desk she had been using while she'd been trying to get into Lee's laptop. She was hunched over with a shocked look on her face. She then looked up, saw Kate, and waved her over with a subtle little motion.

Kate made her way through the small throng of officers and troopers, heading over to the desk. "What is it?" she asked.

"I got in," DeMarco said. "And look at this..."

She had opened a folder with at least one hundred files. DeMarco picked one at random and opened it. It was a video. In it, a woman was on a bed, totally naked, on all fours. Another woman was beside her, stroking the other woman's back, holding what Kate assumed to be a sex toy that she had never seen nor even heard of before.

As if all of that wasn't shocking enough, the next thing that registered in her mind was what did it.

These were not women. These were *young* women. The one on all fours *might* be fifteen or sixteen—right around Mercy Fuller's age.

DeMarco clicked another one. It was another video. This time, there was one female and three males. All of the males looked to be of age—one maybe as old as fifty. The girl, however, was easily underage.

"My God," Kate said, closing the laptop lid. She looked down to DeMarco's face and saw that she was absolutely fuming.

"Kate...that last girl...she couldn't have been older than fourteen."

"I know. Go on outside. Don't even think of going in there with Lee. Catch up to Barnes before he leaves and send him back in here."

DeMarco moved slowly as she did as she was asked. She glanced in the direction of the interrogation room as she walked toward the front doors. Kate saw reporters and camera people still clambering around out there.

One thing after another, after another, Kate thought, looking to Edgar Lee's laptop. *What the hell else could possibly happen today?*

She knew it was a dangerous question because it was barely even noon yet. She got her bearings straight, doing her best to erase the images of those two videos from her mind.

It was a bit easier than she expected because while she did so, her cell phone rang. She took it out of her pocket and saw that it was Melissa. She nearly ignored it, considering everything that was going on. But something in the back of her head said otherwise. *Melissa rarely ever calls you, much less during the day...*

Suddenly, a ball of worry dropped into her stomach. She found herself growing nervous as the phone continued to ring. The flurry of motion around her and the buzzing of reporters outside seemed to make it about one hundred times worse.

She answered the phone, Edgar Lee's laptop suddenly the last thing on her mind. "Hey, Lissa. What's up?"

"I, um...I just wanted you to know that we're at the hospital. It's...it's Michelle. Mom...it might be really bad."

That ball of worry exploded and for a moment, the world seemed to go still. Absolutely motionless. "What is it?" she asked, having to stifle back tears.

"We took her to the doctor yesterday afternoon because she just kept wailing. They couldn't find anything wrong with her and did some blood tests and...we got the results this morning and they sent us straight to the hospital. They think...they think she might have cancer. Neuroblastoma, which I hadn't even heard of and...oh God, Mom...what the hell am I going to do?"

"Do they know for sure?"

"No, not yet. But I think they suspect it. They're running tests right now and they've been giving us the *it's-best-to-be-prepared* talk."

"Neuroblastoma…that's what…that's dealing with the nervous system, right?"

"Yeah. But they're more concerned about how it's presenting. In the abdomen."

"I can be there in about three hours."

"No, Mom. We don't even know for sure yet. I just…I wanted you to know what was going on. Because if it turns out she *does* have it, I didn't want that to be the first call you got, hearing about it."

"When will you know for sure?"

"This is the final test. This is supposed to tell us for certain."

"Let me know, okay? Don't wait. Let me know right away."

She watched the front door as Barnes came in. He looked washed out and in a hurry. His eyes were narrowed with worry. Reporters crowded in behind him. He was headed right for her, a look of absolute defeat on his face.

"Okay, Mom," Melissa said in her ear. "I don't even know if you still do this sort of thing, but would you say a prayer for her? For *us*?"

"Of course I will. I love you, Lissa."

"I love you, too."

She could not remember the last time her daughter had spoken those three words to her. When she ended the call and pocketed her phone, she tried her best to nonchalantly wipe the beginnings of tears away from the corners of her eyes.

Barnes looked at her with a bit of surprise that then dissolved into slight embarrassment. "You okay?" he asked.

"Yeah. What about you? Did DeMarco tell you what we found?"

"She did. But there's something else. Something new. The canine unit called. They found something…and it's not sounding promising."

Before he could even explain to her what information had come across, Kate felt something pass through her head, something like a wind that rocked her balance. She felt lightheaded for a minute as the day's toll caught up with her.

She saw the images from the videos on Edgar Lee's computer.

She heard Melissa's voice, still echoing in her head: *"They think she might have cancer. Neuroblastoma, which I hadn't even heard of..."*

She breathed in deeply, doing her best to re-orient herself.

"Agent Wise?" Barnes was looking at her, concern on his face.

"I'm good," she said, starting for the door before she was fully confident that she could move.

"Agent Wise, if you—"

"Let's go already," she snapped at him, pushing through the door and into the throng of reporters waiting for them outside.

CHAPTER SEVENTEEN

When Barnes turned down the dirt road that Kate now knew was dubbed by the locals as Blood Gulch Road, she had a good idea of where they were headed. She recalled Barnes telling them that there was nothing but woods and a few fields on each side of the road. One of those fields was a particularly large one, called Jones Field.

They arrived at Jones Field by turning down what appeared to be an old logging road of sorts about two miles after they passed the area where Todd Ramsey had found Mercy Fuller's credit card. The road was quite bumpy, but Barnes took it with the ease of a seasoned pro. He stuck mainly to the sides, skipping the vast majority of the dips and holes. It took three minutes of this driving to reach the edge of the field. Several state police cars were scattered here and there at the edge of the road and at the opening to the large field.

The field itself was mostly bare, covered in weeds and wildflowers. A few stubborn trees broke the plainness, looking sorely out of place in the middle of the field. From the few police cars to the other side of the field, Kate estimated there was about a quarter of a mile or so of open space. Slightly to the right of center, about two hundred feet away, several state policemen with the canine unit were huddled in a semicircle. Kate, DeMarco, and Foster hurried out to meet with them, wading through the tall grass to get there.

When she joined the group in the field, she saw that whoever had pushed the state PD to get out here with the canine unit had also sent someone with forensics. He was holding a plastic evidence bag in his hands. Inside was a thin Under Armour windbreaker, light blue in color. A smattering of blood adorned one of the sleeves.

"What is that?" she asked. She flashed her badge as if it were an afterthought.

The guy from forensics—Brent Halloway, according to the lanyard he wore—gave Kate's badge a once-over before responding. She noted that he also wore a digital SLR camera around his neck.

"A windbreaker, size small," Halloway said. "From the looks of it, it hasn't been out here long. The blood on the sleeve is dry, but relatively fresh."

"Were there pictures taken before it was bagged?" Kate asked.

"Certainly," Halloway said. He handed the bag to the cop closest to him and then took the camera off of his neck. He started rolling back through several pictures until he came to one of the windbreaker as it had been found. As Kate looked at it, Halloway walked her and DeMarco through several of the details.

"There's also blood on the bottom of it, but not a lot. Also, if you noticed the way most of the fabric on the sleeves is sort of wrinkled and bunched up, it leads me to believe that the victim wasn't actually wearing it. She may have had it tied around her waist like kids do sometimes."

She looked to Barnes, showing him the picture. "I don't suppose you knew the Fuller family well enough to know if this would have belonged to Mercy, do you?"

"Sorry, no," he said. "But that does look like a color a girl would wear, doesn't it?"

Kate nodded and then lowered her head as she spoke to DeMarco. She spoke quietly, wanting to keep things between them just for the moment. "Do me a favor. Call Anne Pettus and ask if she can confirm if Mercy owned a light blue Under Armour windbreaker."

DeMarco nodded and then walked away from the little group, wandering several yards further to the right into the overgrown weeds.

Kate handed the phone back to Halloway and took several steps away from the area the clothing had been discovered. She looked out into the field and saw several areas where the grass and weeds appeared to have been recently passed through.

"Looks like some messed up maze, doesn't it?" Barnes asked from behind her.

"It does," she said. She counted at least fifteen different trampled areas, none of which were pressed down hard enough to have been done so with any real force.

"Most of it is likely just deer," Barnes said. "Hell, we've even had black bears spotted around Deton recently."

"One of them had to have been made by whoever owned that windbreaker," Kate said. "And whoever was with them. I'm going to see if I can find any footprints of any kind along the ground in those areas. Think you can get some more eyes on this for me?"

"I'm on it," Barnes said, stepping away.

No sooner had he left her did DeMarco step up beside her, taking his place. "I spoke with Anne. She said she's almost positive Mercy had a light blue jacket or windbreaker of some kind. She's looking through pictures on her phone to try to find one where Mercy is wearing it."

"That would certainly be helpful."

"Anything useful out here?" DeMarco asked. But the way she was looking out to the wide open field and the several faint depressions in the tall grass told Kate that she already knew the answer.

"It's a needle in a haystack scenario right now," Kate answered. "I think if we—"

The sound of an incoming text on DeMarco's phone cut her off. DeMarco took her phone out quickly. As she looked at it, she said: "It's Anne."

She held her phone out in front of them and opened up the text. There were no words, just two pictures. One showed only Anne and Mercy. Another showed the two girls with several other young girls. In both of them, Mercy was wearing a light blue Under Armour zip-up windbreaker. It was identical to the one in Brent Halloway's bag.

"Well, I suppose the good news is that we can now rule Mercy Fuller out as the murderer of her parents," Kate said.

"And the bad," DeMarco added, "is that we have no idea where Mercy is. We don't even know if she's alive or dead."

Kate realized that this case had now become what she had dreaded from the start. They were not only on the lookout for killer...but they needed to find a fifteen-year-old girl before her abductor took things too far and killed her as well. And if history had taught her anything about these cases, it was that Mercy's chances of being found alive became smaller with each minute that passed.

CHAPTER EIGHTEEN

By one o'clock that afternoon, the town of Deton, Virginia, was overcrowded with police cars. There were more from the state sent in to assist with what was now officially being referred to as a murder and abduction case. There were plenty of officers coming in from Richmond, and Barnes had essentially committed every Deton officer to the case.

While Jones Field and all of Blood Gulch Road was being combed over by a total of fifteen officers, Kate and DeMarco were at the Deton police station. They were sitting in the conference room again, this time with Barnes, Foster, and now Brent Halloway. Barnes was currently putting the finishing touches on the last piece of tape to keep a huge area map of Deton and most of the surrounding area, including Deerfield, up on the wall. While he'd done this, Foster had brought it an old whiteboard. It was clear that the station was not used to handling cases like this but Kate admired the grit and determination of the small-town police in making sure they remained as thorough as possible despite their lack of resources.

"Agent Wise, this is your show," Barnes said, stepping aside from the map.

"I appreciate that," she said. "But can you stay right up there and draw us a line that runs from the Fuller residence to Jones Field?"

Barnes grabbed a Sharpie from the table and leaned in toward the map. He drew a circle and tapped it. "This is the Fuller residence, give or take a mile or so," he said. He scanned the map again and drew another circle within five seconds. "And here's Jones Field."

He drew a line connecting the two. It covered a pretty good chunk of ground, a fact Kate knew would make their search even harder.

"How much real estate is that?" DeMarco asked.

"I'd guess about twelve miles between the house and the field. But if you're talking an entire area, covering all the ground between the two, I don't know. The back roads are pretty straight and all snake back around to the same points, but that's a lot of forest."

"Agents," Officer Foster said, "can I ask what the assumption is, based on the discovery of Mercy Fuller's bloodstained windbreaker?"

"Well, as I told Agent DeMarco out at Jones Field," Kate said, "this basically tells us that Mercy Fuller did not kill her parents and skip town. She's now officially the epicenter of this case, and it needs to be quick, Not only because we have no idea who has her or where she is, but because she's apparently been wounded and is bleeding."

"I hate to be the grim one here," Barnes said, "but I feel like the discovery of blood on clothes means she's likely already dead."

"That's a reasonable assumption," Kate said. "But it doesn't quite fit. She was abducted for some reason—whether sexual, domination fantasy, some grief with the family, whatever it may be. If she was indeed dead, I feel like we would have also found her body with the windbreaker. A dead abductee doesn't serve much of a purpose."

"So you think she's alive?" Foster asked.

"I have no idea. But I do think she was very much alive when that windbreaker was dropped. I also dare to think she might have dropped it on purpose. Mr. Halloway here says that the sleeves were crumpled in a way that indicates they might have been tied together around her waist. I think Mercy Fuller might have left it behind on purpose, without her abductor realizing, hoping to leave a useable clue behind."

"So where do we go from here?" Barnes asked.

"I think we can likely limit the search to the area along that line you just drew. If the abductor went through Jones Field, they likely did it to avoid main roads. He's a local. He knows the area."

Barnes nodded, but he didn't look so certain. He looked back to the map, his shoulders hunched and his eyes distant.

"Sheriff, you can say whatever it is that's on your mind," Kate said.

"The blood…and then the field and all of these damned woods. What if we're using all of this manpower to look for a girl that's already dead?"

"Even if that *is* the case," DeMarco said, clearly a little irritated at the defeatist attitude, "that mean there's a girl's body out there somewhere and she would deserve to be found and properly taken care of."

"And we can't afford to think like that," Kate said, getting to her feet. "Unless we find a corpse, we work as if Mercy Fuller is still alive."

As she said this, a thought occurred to her. Some old memory from her past came bubbling to the surface. The memory was hazy, but she could remember the case it was pulled from.

"Excuse me a second, would you?"

With that, she got up and left the room. As she closed the door, she focused on the memory, making sure it didn't slip away. She grinned half-heartedly, wondering if her fear of not being able to hold onto distant memories was related to the fact that she was fifty-six years old or if her mind was simply crammed full of similar memories from her illustrious career.

She took out her cell phone and pulled up a number she had not even thought about in nearly a year. She looked at the name before calling, that same thin smile on her face.

Jimmy Parker. She had, of course, spoken to Parker for a bit when she had been asked to return to the bureau on something of a part-time basis. Between Parker and the partner she'd had for the last eight years of her career, a younger guy named Logan Nash, she had plenty of invaluable resources to pull from. But in that moment, she thought of Jimmy Parker. He'd been with her during this memory in her head and, besides that, the man was the sort of older man—in his sixties now—who seemed to enjoy doling out insights.

She sent the call, fully expecting him to ignore it. However, she also knew that if he saw her name on the display (assuming he still had her number saved) he'd likely jump at the opportunity to speak with her.

When the call was answered on the second ring, she was delighted. Not only because he had taken the call, but to be able to hear his voice again.

"My caller ID reads *Kate Wise*," Parker said. "But that can't be right. Kate Wise was re-recruited to the bureau and is out catching bad guys."

"Hi to you, too, Jimmy."

"Kate. How are you? To what do I owe the pleasure?"

"Well, I hate to be hasty, but you weren't too far off from the truth. I *am* out trying to catch a bad guy and this moment popped up in my head. Back in the early nineties, I think it was. You and I were out west somewhere…in Kansas, I think. A missing persons case involving two men. But the details just won't come to me."

"That would be the Tremblay case. I don't recall the name of the town but it was one of those rustic farming communities. Two brothers got into a squabble and one killed the other. The one that survived ran off, taking his brother's kid with him."

84

"Yeah. That's the one. It popped up in my head as we were going over this current missing persons case and I can't really figure out why."

"What are the details?"

She quickly went through the higher-level details of the Fuller case, giving him a brief summation in about twenty seconds. When she was done, Parker chuckled. "Man, I can't believe you forgot about that case."

"Why? What am I missing?"

"Well, you're the one that sort of broke it, if I remember correctly. Can you remember who we chased after for several days before we realized it was the brother that did it?"

"The brother's wife. There were clues and leads everywhere that told us it was her. But in the end it was the brother. It took us…"

"I take it the pause means you're making some sort of connection?" Parker asked.

"But with this case, the parents are both dead."

"Does that really matter? You've been digging into the daughter's life, looking for ways to understand her. But what if you checked out the parents instead?"

"That's just it. We have, for the most part. No local family, no arrest records, no…"

She stopped here. She saw where he was trying to lead her. And while she had vaguely gone there herself, the immediacy of finding Mercy Fuller had torn her away from it. Now, though, able to talk it out with an old partner, it started to make more sense.

"What if the parents were somehow involved in the whole thing?" she asked almost to herself.

"I wouldn't go there right away either," Parker said. "Based on what you've told me, it would be far from the natural inclination, but you know as well as I do that the people you have no reason to suspect are sometimes the most interesting ones."

"Thanks for this, Parker."

"No need to thank me. You would have figured it out for yourself before too long. Besides…you have a family and a life outside of all of this. I retired and returned home to pretty much nothing. All this time to myself…I tend to dive back into case notes and old memories of the job far too often."

"You can always come pay me a visit in Richmond."

"I might just do that one day."

Kate wrapped the call and walked back into the conference room. She sat back down among a conversation about the possible

85

routes the abductor could have taken through the woods and where those routes would come out. Barnes and Foster bickered about it a bit before leaving the floor open.

"Sheriff Barnes, has anyone looked into Wendy or Alvin Fuller?" she asked. "Maybe about their histories and who they may have known that could be responsible?"

It was Foster who answered. He replied quickly, both eager to help and seemingly offended that she thought they'd miss something so clear. It was apparent in his tone and the gaze he cast her way when he spoke.

"It was the first thing we looked into. It was rather easy, though. Both of Alvin's parents are dead. Wendy's mother is still alive but she lives in Connecticut somewhere. We asked friends of the family and even sent someone down to Charlotte County to speak to Alvin's two brothers."

"Anything on the brothers?" DeMarco asked.

"The older one did some small time for drugs a few years ago. Nothing serious."

"Can we get whatever files you have on the Fullers, their friends, and relatives?" Kate asked.

Foster gave a nod and stood up from the table. Kate then looked over to Halloway, who was scrolling through pictures of Jones Field on his phone. "Halloway, do you think you could get us whatever the state PD has on the murder scene?"

Without looking up from his phone, he slid the photo gallery away and pulled up his email. "I'll shoot an email right now. I suspect we'll have it within ten or fifteen minutes."

"With all due respect," Barnes said, showing perhaps his first signs of doubt, "Wendy and Alvin Fuller are dead. What can you possibly hope to find by looking into their pasts?"

"I don't know just yet," she said. She then added what Parker had told her on the phone, that almost cheesy saying that, in the moment, seemed to be pointing her in the right direction. "But when it comes to cracking a case where there are no direct witnesses, the people you have no reason to suspect are sometimes the most interesting ones."

CHAPTER NINETEEN

Kate and DeMarco were given the conference room to use as a makeshift office. For the remainder of the afternoon, they set up at the table, sending off for file requests from the Deton PD, the state police, and the bureau. Duran worked diligently behind the scenes to acquire an intern agent to fetch whatever they needed right away, sending the information to Deton either via email or direct calls.

By four o'clock that afternoon, Kate had a pretty good picture of both Wendy and Alvin Fuller. DeMarco had even gone so far as to write some of their notes on the whiteboard Foster had brought in earlier. While they had a portrait of the Fullers, Kate knew that they'd have to go deeper to find anything worthwhile.

That's why they now had bank statements, cell phone bills, and the contact information of their employers dating back to several years before they were even married. Even now, as Kate and DeMarco pored over all of the files they had gathered up in the last several hours, Barnes came into the room, carrying another small stack.

"We've officially managed to speak to all five people that Alvin Fuller has ever worked for, with the exception of the manager of the video rental place he worked at in college but that's only because he died four years ago. They all said Alvin was perfectly fine, just a little on the quiet side."

"Where did he go to college?" Kate asked.

"Oh, that's right here," DeMarco said, holding up one her sheets of paper. "VCU. He attended for two years before dropping out."

"Any idea how Wendy and Alvin met, Sheriff?" Kate asked.

"No idea. They didn't always live here. Came into town about fifteen years or so ago. Right when little Mercy was a baby."

"Any idea why they moved here?"

"Not really. I knew they were from somewhere around the Roanoke area. I always figured it was easier for a family to get by on very little money out here. Alvin had a good job at the lumber mill out in Deerfield. Around here, it's not a job to sneeze at, you know?"

"Do you know if he had that job since the first day? Maybe he moved here specifically for that job?"

"No, I asked that when I spoke to his boss. According to them, their records show that he applied for the job *after* coming to Deton. So if he moved here for a specific reason, it wasn't that. And while I do love my town, it's not really the sort of place people move to just for the hell of it, you know?"

"And his employer there said nothing was out of the ordinary, right?"

"Right. He was just as shocked as anyone."

As Barnes stepped back out of the room, Kate reclined back in her seat a bit and landed on a particular thought. It didn't seem important per se, but it did seem a little odd. She spoke out it out loud to DeMarco, hoping they could figure it out between them.

"So why would a married couple with a baby that wasn't even one year old yet move to a place like this if there wasn't already a steady job lined up?"

"That *does* seem weird," DeMarco said. "Maybe they were trying to get away from something?"

"Maybe." What she didn't say out loud was: *And if they were running from something, did it come all the way to Deton fifteen years later to catch up to them?*

***

At some point, someone ordered pizza and someone else put on a pot of coffee. When Foster came into the room to offer them pizza, Kate looked to her watch and was surprised to find that it had somehow come to be 6:30. She stood up and stretched, realizing that she could indeed go for a few slices of pizza.

Another officer came in behind Foster and handed over a single sheet of paper. Kate took it and saw that it was one of the several documents she had asked for when this whole Fuller excavation had started. It was a copy of Wendy and Alvin Fuller's marriage certificate. They'd been married twenty-one years ago, at an old vineyard-based colonial retreat in Waynesboro, Virginia.

"This is great," Kate said, though it didn't really tell them much of anything. "How are we looking on those medical records?"

"We have some, but they seem to be coming from all over the place. We've got some from, Lynchburg, Charlottesville, and the local doctor here in Deton. The office in Lynchburg has notes on their files that all records were requested to be transferred to a doctor's office in Waynesboro due to a move. They haven't sent us anything just yet."

"Can you bring me the number? I'll convince them to move a little faster."

The officer smiled and gave a nod as he turned on his heel and left.

"You think medical records are even worth looking into?" DeMarco asked as they left the room in search of pizza.

"No idea," Kate answered. "But if they were running from something, it might not necessarily be someone or some legal trouble. It could be sentimental or emotional reasons. Or medical reasons. I just don't want to leave any stones unturned."

They found the pizza in the bullpen area. While they were there, plating pizza and grabbing sodas that had also been brought in, Kate was able to catch up on the most up to date information about the case—information she was being told anyway but was constantly circulating through the building like some primitive form of social media.

She discovered that the canine unit had found nothing else of interest since coming across the windbreaker. They'd nearly gotten excited for a split second when one of the dogs had led them to a partial shape buried slightly in the foliage of the forest, but it had turned out to be a deer carcass.

She also learned that because of the heavy state involvement, the story was now on the news. Upon hearing this, Kate looked out the front doors and the picture window at the front of the building and saw without much surprise that there were numerous news vans out there.

As she and DeMarco made their way back to their makeshift office, the officer who had been tasked with collecting medical records stopped her. He handed her a slip of paper with two numbers on it.

"The first one is the direct line. It's after hours, so you'll be asked to press One and you can leave a message for emergencies. I already did that and so far, I have nothing. The second number is the one I was given for their records department."

"Thanks," Kate said, taking the slip of paper.

She reentered their workspace, placed her pizza on the table, and tried the first number. As the officer had told her, it went to a recorded message after just two rings. She waited patiently; she knew if it came down to it, she could call DC and have someone find the name and number of the primary physician and call them directly. But by the time all of that was taken care of, she felt she could probably get someone on the phone herself.

She left a message, very aware that DeMarco was sitting there listening to her. She wanted to really lay into it, the express the urgency in a way that might be borderline unprofessional, but she relented.

"This is Agent Kate Wise with the FBI," she said. "I'm currently in Deton, Virginia, working on the Fuller case, which I'm sure by now someone at your office has seen on the news. I need access to the medical records you have on file for Wendy and Alvin Fuller. I'd like to keep it calm and cordial—just between us. But if I don't get a call back very soon, I'm afraid I'll have to expedite things by getting my director on your heels."

She left her number and ended the call. DeMarco was grinning at her as she started on a slice of pizza. "I bet you're absolutely horrifying when you're actually *mad*."

"Let's hope you never have to see that," Kate said.

They finished up their pizza and once again started to sift through all of the information that had come in so far. Officer Foster had even started collecting the names and numbers of any kids that went to Mercy's school that might have come into contact with Alvin and Wendy. They were looking for any thread at all, no matter how stretched and vague, to lead them to their next clues.

It was 7:17 when Kate's phone rang. She was digging through the police records of extended family (and coming up with basically nothing) when the ringing broke her concentration. In the back of her mind, she was hoping it would be Melissa, giving her an update on Michelle. Because of this nerve-inducing situation, Kate didn't even bother looking at the number on the caller display.

"This is Agent Wise," she answered.

"Hi, Agent Wise. This is Theresa McKinney, one of the head practitioners here at Waynesboro Family Medicine, returning your call."

"Good to hear from you. What do we need to do to get those records?"

"Just standard practice. I'd need your badge number, the name of your direct supervisor, and the best way to get the records to you. Typically we'd need more details about the case as well but, as you said, it's pretty much been all over the news."

Kate gave her what she needed, rattling off her badge number and then her email address. McKinney was helpful enough but, perhaps because of her loyalty to her patients and her oath as a doctor, didn't seem too happy about so willingly handing over such private information.

After the call, Kate had Sheriff Barnes bring her in a laptop so she wouldn't have to look through medical records on her phone. Her eyesight was not at all what it once was and even for someone with perfect eyesight, looking through official documents on a phone screen was never an easy task.

Five minutes later, she had a laptop connected to the department's network and printing out medical records for Alvin and Wendy Fuller as far back as twenty years ago. The volumes were slim; it appeared Alvin had only been to the doctor three times over the span of about five years and each visit had been something relatively minor: the flu, a sinus infection, and a sprained ankle.

Wendy Fuller's file was a little thicker, though not by much. She tended to have a lot of migraines, from what Kate was seeing. Other than that, there wasn't much of note.

Not until the last three pages. The final page listed a visit for a series of tests. It took Kate a while to dance around the medical jargon, but she was fairly certain these were tests that Wendy Fuller had asked to have done—not ones that had been suggested by an MD. They were mostly blood tests for something called FSH, but there was also a referral to see a specialist.

"DeMarco...there's a medical abbreviation here...FSH. It sounds familiar but I can't for the life of me pull it to memory."

"FSH...isn't that something to do with fertility?" She whipped out her phone like it was a magic wand and typed the abbreviation into Google. It took less than three seconds for her to get the result. "FSH. Follicle-stimulating hormone. It says here that FSH can help in preparing a woman's eggs for release each month."

Kate nodded as she flipped to the next page. This was a copy of a record from another doctor—presumably the specialist that Waynesboro Family Medicine had referred Wendy Fuller to. There was a lot of medical terminology that went over Kate's head but there was a list of tests that told her quite a bit: hormone tests, ovulation testing, assorted fertility treatments...

"Look at this," Kate said, slipping it over to DeMarco. "It looks like Wendy Fuller had concerns about her fertility. And if you check the date, it looks like all of these tests and treatments were recommended about a year before Mercy was born."

"Seems like a happy story to me, then," DeMarco said. "Whatever tests they felt Wendy needed obviously worked."

"That was my first thought, too. But the math doesn't work. Her first appointment was just a little over a year before Mercy was born. That would mean she had questions and concerns about fertility just three months before Mercy would have been

91

conceived. And I don't know that any sort of treatment would take after only two or three months."

"That *does* seem weird, doesn't it?"

Kate looked over the final page of the records. It was from Staunton Women's Services, the finer print stating it was a form from the office of Dr. Beatrice Dudley, a reproductive endocrinologist. Kate had no idea what that title meant so, like DeMarco, she looked it up on her phone. Apparently, a reproductive endocrinologist was a fertility specialist who also served primarily, in most cases, as an OBGYN.

But that was where the trail stopped. There was nothing else following the visit to the specialist. Whatever the results were, they were not here in the files. Sure, the fact that the Fullers eventually had a daughter basically told the story, but the fact that the trail came to such an abrupt end seemed peculiar to Kate.

"I've worked with you enough to know that face," DeMarco said. "You're hatching a plan, aren't you?"

"I am. How do you feel about taking a trip out to Waynesboro?"

"Tonight?"

Kate nodded, staring at Wendy Fuller's medical files. "I think going back to the town they lived in before they had Mercy makes the most sense. We can visit the Women's Services place in Staunton and maybe talk to some people that knew them when they lived there."

"I could be up for a late-night road trip. Just let me grab a cup of coffee."

"Grab me one, too, please," she said.

As DeMarco left, Kate gathered up all of the records they had accumulated through the latter part of the day. As she started sorting them out into file folders, she couldn't help but feel that there was some big answer buried in it all—and that it could very well be hidden somewhere in the Fullers' old stomping grounds.

CHAPTER TWENTY

The drive between Deton and Staunton took less than an hour, so Kate and DeMarco were able to relocate without doing so in the middle of the night. They checked in to a Best Western shortly after nine, checked in with Duran back in DC, and found themselves sitting in a motel room with a recorded history of the last final twenty years or so of Wendy and Alvin Fuller printed out before them.

Just as Kate was beginning to go back through all of the medical records, fully prepared to Google each and every test that had been suggested for Wendy Fuller, her phone rang. When she saw Melissa's name on the display, she felt like her heart was beating. It was one of those moments where she knew that the call would either bring news so relieving that it would make her feel like she was floating, or so bad that her world would probably never be the same again.

"Hey, Lissa," she said as she answered the phone. "Do you know anything yet?"

"We just got home. Mom, they did so many tests…all day. But they couldn't find anything to show that she definitively has cancer. There's some blood work that needs to come back, but from what I understand, if what they saw today didn't show anything, we can breathe easy."

"But we're not one hundred percent certain yet?"

"No. Not one hundred percent. We'll get the results of the last batch of blood work tomorrow, and they want us to come in next week for a follow-up. But the doctor in charge of her case said that he's not worried, based on what he saw today."

"That's great news."

"It is. We're um…well, we're very thankful. It was scary as hell, but we know it could have been a lot worse."

"Will you keep me posted if anything else pops up?"

"Of course."

"And I'll come by and visit when I get back in town. I have no idea when that will be, but—"

"It's okay, Mom. We're good. I just wanted to give you an update so you wouldn't be worrying about us all night."

"Thanks for the call. Let me know if you need anything."

They hung up, leaving Kate to look at the mound of information on the Fullers. It was the first time since coming back from Jones Field when Kate wasn't sure if she was in the right place. The "right place" right now felt like wherever Melissa and Michelle were.

"Everything okay?" DeMarco asked.

"Yeah. Just feeling like a guilty grandmother."

"Any particular reason why?"

Kate sighed, fully prepared to keep it from DeMarco. It wouldn't have been out of any sort of secretive reasons—but mainly because she didn't want to hinder her partner with her own personal issues. But she then recalled the conversation they'd had the previous night, where DeMarco had opened up a bit about her own personal life.

"Melissa had a pretty bad scare today," she answered. "With Michelle. Everything is okay now, but it was frightening for a while there."

She went on to tell DeMarco about what Melissa had been through today—and in turn, what she had been dealing with in the background while they had been hunting down answers regarding the Fullers. It didn't take long and she was surprised to find that it was easier to talk to DeMarco about it than she had originally thought.

"So you've had that weight on your shoulders all afternoon?" DeMarco asked.

"Yeah."

DeMarco chuckled and said, "You're a stronger woman than I am, that's for sure."

Kate took the compliment, but she doubted it was a true comment. She knew DeMarco had a mean streak inside of her. It was a streak she had seen glimpses of whenever the issue of child abuse of any kind had come up in their line of work.

It was an unspoken thing, but her sharing the news about Michelle seemed to put a bow on the night. Without saying as much, they both got ready for bed. And when Kate lay down in the darkness of the motel room, she said a little prayer for her granddaughter. Even at fifty-six, she was still not sure where she rested with the whole God-thing, but she assumed it never hurt to pray—to God, to the universe, or whatever might be out there listening.

And with that prayer said, she was able to fall asleep with only the weight of the Fuller case on her shoulders.

***

They started the following morning at the Staunton Women's Services building. It was primarily what Kate had always referred to as the lady doctor. When she and DeMarco walked in, she spotted three visibly pregnant women right away. They skipped by the check-in windows and went straight to the last window on the right, where a sign above it read, simply: Information.

Kate subtly slid her badge and ID across the counter. "We were in contact with Waynesboro Family Medicine yesterday concerning a time-sensitive case," she explained to the woman on the other side of the window. "They sent us records for a woman named Wendy Fuller. Her last medical record before she and her husband moved was a visit here, as a referral from her doctor. Who could we speak to in regards to those kinds of records?"

The woman behind the desk typed into her computer and then narrowed her brow. *She's probably realizing that we're looking into records that are sixteen years old,* Kate thought.

"In terms of the records end of things, I don't know how much help we can be," the woman said. "However, the doctor that was seeing Mrs. Fuller is still on staff. She's working today, as a matter of fact. She's with a patient right now, but I can see if she can meet with you immediately afterwards."

"That would be great," Kate said.

Kate and DeMarco were directed to sit in a secondary waiting room, likely not to stand out among a waiting room of expectant mothers or women who were already uneasy from any number of invasive exams.

"Something occurred to me on the drive here this morning," DeMarco said. "If the Fullers were indeed running away from something—and that's why they made the move from Waynesboro to Deton—why not move further away? The towns are only about fifty miles apart."

It was a good question, and one that Kate had no answers to. She was hoping it would be one of the questions they could answer while visiting Staunton and Waynesboro. "Any theories yet?" Kate asked.

Just as DeMarco shook her head, a nurse came in through one of the doors to the side of the room. She looked around for a moment, spotted Kate and DeMarco and then waved them forward. The agents joined her at the door and followed her down a small hallway.

"You'll be meeting with Dr. Amy Shilling," the nurse said. "I believe she's pulling up the records you were asking about earlier."

She led them to the end of the hallway and then to the right at a small T-intersection. She gestured to the first room along this hallway. The door was open, revealing a woman in a white doctor's gown sitting behind a desk, looking at something on a laptop. She looked up as Kate knocked softly on the door.

"Dr. Shilling?" Kate asked.

"That's me. You're the agents, I assume?"

They ran through a quick round of introductions as Shilling invited them to take two of the three seats in front of her desk.

"So, I have the records here on Wendy Fuller. The last thing I have for her is a series of tests that she underwent at the suggestion of her family MD. That was sixteen years ago. Does that sound right to you?"

"That's the time table, for sure," Kate said.

"And while we aren't even sure these records would have anything to do with what we're looking for, exactly," DeMarco said, "we're trying to get the broadest picture possible."

"Can I ask what this is about?" Shilling asked.

"We can't reveal the minute details, but the broader picture is on the news. Wendy and her husband were murdered a few days ago. In their home in Deton, Virginia."

"Oh my goodness," Shilling said. "Though I suppose the move explains why this is the last record I have on her."

"Do you recall her at all?" Kate asked.

"Not specifically. I see many women for infertility concerns."

"I figured you'd remember her because she was a success story," DeMarco said.

"Excuse me?"

"Well, she did end up having a daughter. Mercy Fuller."

"When was that?" Shilling asked.

"It would have been about a year after she met with you."

As Kate listened to the exchange, she realize that something was very much off here. She could see it in Shilling's expression. She could hear it in DeMarco's quickly suspicious tone.

"Well, this record shows that we conducted the tests," Shilling said. "It also shows that we got the results of all of them but we were never able to contact Mrs. Fuller. From what it says here, we never got in touch with her. We called and emailed, but there was never anything. No word from her at all."

"So she never got the results?" Kate asked.

"No. It's almost as if she didn't want to hear it."

"And what *were* the results, Dr. Shilling?" DeMarco asked.

"Well, that's why I'm so confused about this daughter of hers. According to the tests we got back, Wendy Fuller was very much infertile."

CHAPTER TWENTY ONE

Kate left Staunton Women's Services reeling. The enormous piece of the puzzle they had received from Dr. Shilling made absolutely no sense. And it drastically altered the course of the case. It was such a blow to the case that Kate and DeMarco sat in the car, remaining in the parking lot, for several minutes after leaving the building.

"How's this even possible?" DeMarco asked.

"Common sense points towards adoption," Kate answered. "But if there was anything related to adoption—or even foster care, for that matter—there would have been something in the public records we pulled back in Deton."

"So...where the hell did Mercy Fuller come from?"

"That's a damned good question."

Kate reached into the back seat of the car and gathered up her files on Wendy and Alvin Fuller. There wasn't much about their lives in Waynesboro—just a ten-minute jaunt from Staunton—so they didn't have much to filter through.

"We've got an old address for the Fullers and the last known employer for Alvin before the move. Coleman Furniture and Cabinets in Waynesboro."

"Seems like that's our next stop, then," DeMarco said.

Kate felt like they were grasping at straws at this point. The revelation that Wendy Fuller had been infertile blew the case apart, leaving no clear direction of where to go. But they had come out here hoping to dig up some answers. They sure as hell had gotten one; it just so happened that this particular answer brought many more questions with it.

***

Waynesboro was slightly larger than Deton. With an actual Main Street, courthouse, and a few storefronts, it seemed like a metropolis in comparison. The place still boasted a population of under three thousand, making the traffic at 9:30 in the morning nearly nonexistent.

They found Coleman Furniture and Cabinets at the far end of town, alone on its own little plot of land. A small lumber scrapyard sat behind the property, as well as a few small sheds. It was apparently the kind of place that built its own furniture—something that seemed to tie directly into Alvin Fuller's eventual job in Deton as a foreman at the lumber yard.

They walked into the central building, which was quite large and boasted several display set-ups of custom-built cabinets and handcrafted living room furniture. They had only been inside for about ten seconds before a cheerful woman came down one of the large open aisles to greet them.

"Can I help you ladies?" she asked.

"Yes, actually," Kate said. "We were wondering if the manager might happen to be here? Or, if not a manager, someone that might be able to help us with finding information on a former employee."

The woman was clearly a little baffled but didn't miss a beat. With a thin smile, she said: "That would be Mr. Coleman—Sam Coleman. He's owned and operated the business for over twenty-five years. And, because he's a creature of habit, he is indeed in his office right now. Can I tell him who's asking for him?"

"We're with the FBI," DeMarco said. "We just need to see if he can help us out with finding some information about someone who used to work here."

"Oh, I see. Well, right this way. I'm sure he'd be happy to help."

The lady led them through the store, one display after another until they came to the back. She led them back behind the large counter and down a small hallway. One large room occupied most of the right side of the hall, an office where a slightly overweight older man sat behind a desk. He was partially hidden by an ancient-looking Dell desktop monitor.

"Mr. Coleman?" the cheerful lady said. "You've got some visitors."

The older man looked away from the computer and gave them a pleasant smile. Kate guessed him to be closing in on seventy. He had puffy cheeks and a thin white beard that reminded her a bit of her own grandfather.

"And who can I help?" he asked, smiling.

The floor saleslady took her leave, heading back out toward the counter. Kate and DeMarco stepped in and underwent their usual round of introductions.

"FBI?" Coleman asked. "My goodness, whatever for?"

"We were hoping to get some information on a man who worked here nearly twenty years ago. He and his wife moved away from Waynesboro to Deton, Virginia. We need to find information on their lives previous to the move."

Coleman nodded his head in the direction of an old filing cabinet that sat tucked away in the corner. With a grunt, he got to his feet and walked over to it.

"We've been open for twenty-eight years," he said. "And we pride ourselves with our employee turnover rate. Very few people have ever quit. I think in total, we've had only twenty-two different people work here for us, and that includes the craftsmen. Who is it you're looking for?"

"Alvin Fuller."

"Oh yes, I remember Alvin," Coleman said, opening up one of the cabinets and fishing through it. "A nice enough man, but I really don't think he was ever truly happy here."

"What do you remember about him?" DeMarco asked.

"Well, he was always good for a joke. He wasn't like a clown or anything, but he was always trying to make people laugh." He selected a file, took it out, and handed it to Kate. "He was a good man. He was a young guy when he was here. Got the job right after he and his wife got married, I believe."

Kate flipped through the file folder. There was very little to see: Alvin's application, his resume, a single work-accident report, old insurance information, and three years' worth of W2s.

"Do you know why he moved?" Kate asked.

"He never did tell us. He was very hush-hush about it. I figured he was maybe going across the country or something. To hear he moved here to go somewhere like Deton is sort of strange to me."

"Any problem with him while he was working here?"

"Not a single one that I can remember."

"Did you ever meet his wife?" DeMarco asked. "Her name was Wendy."

"No. Afraid not."

"Do you maybe ever remember him mentioning that his wife had gotten pregnant?"

"No, I don't. But now that I think back on it, it wasn't just that I sometimes got the feeling that he wasn't happy here. Near the end, I always thought he seemed sort of distracted...sad, maybe. Like his mind was on something else."

Kate considered all of this, nodding slightly. She exchanged a look with DeMarco and they got to their feet at the same time. "Mr. Coleman, do you mind if I snap a few pictures of these documents in his file?"

"No, that's fine. Can I ask...is Alvin okay?"

Kate then broke the news of what had happened. She left the office, asking Mr. Coleman to please contact her if he thought of anything else. As they took their leave, she thought she saw a sad look on the old man's face as he peered back into the past and, perhaps, wondered if he had missed some essential clue regarding the mental state of a former employee.

***

Following a mostly fruitless trip to Coleman Furniture and Cabinets, Kate headed back toward Main Street and located the police station. Like most of the other buildings along this little stretch, there was plenty of parking out front and very little foot traffic along the side of the street. When they entered the little police station, Kate was grateful that there were no scrambling reporters or idling new vans to slow her progress. It made her thankful to be away from the headache of Deton, even if for only a day.

With the unexpected mystery of Wendy Fuller's infertility, Kate felt as if she was being pushed as she entered the station. She made a direct line to the small reception desk sitting almost centered several yards away from the front door. Before the officer at the desk could so much as look up to them, Kate was already talking.

"We're Agents Wise and DeMarco, with the FBI," Kate said, flashing her ID. "I need to speak with someone associated with records to get details on two former Waynesboro residents."

The officer seemed to catch the urgency behind Kate's words and wasted no time in assisting. She paged someone elsewhere in the station and in less than a minute, another officer was leading them back into the station. As they made their way to what Kate assumed was the records room, another officer appeared from around the corner. Not just an officer, Kate noted when she saw the man's badge on his chest.

"I'm Deputy Rothbridge," he said in a thick southern accent. He looked to be about fifty or so, a grayed moustache and chiseled chin making him look like a younger Sam Elliot. "Anything I can do to help?"

"Maybe," Kate said. The other officer stopped in front of a door, opened it for them, and then gestured inside with a quick nod. He gave Deputy Rothbridge a rather excited look as he passed back by them, headed back the way he had come.

"Have you heard about the double murder and possible abduction over in Deton?" DeMarco asked.

"I have. You working that?"

"We are," Kate said. "And as it turns out, the victims once lived in Waynesboro. They moved to Deton about fifteen years ago. We're trying to figure out why. There are details emerging that we can't quite share just yet, but we're hoping there might be some information here on Wendy and Alvin Fuller that can make things a bit clearer."

"Well, the names don't ring any bells," Rothbridge said. "But you're welcome to look at anything you need to." He had already walked over to one of the two laptops sitting on a desk against the wall. He typed in a password and waited for the desktop to come up. "We went fully digital about five years ago," he said. "If you *do* need anything else you can't find here or in these old cabinets, let me know."

He hovered around a bit as Kate and DeMarco sat down by the laptop. Kate, fully aware that DeMarco was much better with all things computer-related, let her partner have the seat at the keyboard.

It took a few instructional cues from Rothbridge for DeMarco to get into the database but once she was in, she found what she needed easily enough. But, as Kate had feared, there was very little to be found on the Fullers. Alvin had gotten a speeding ticket and had gone to court to protest it. He also had two parking tickets, both on Main Street. There was also a form on file that seemed to be nothing more than a means to verify their old physical address here in Waynesboro.

And that was it. Or so it seemed at first.

"Deputy," DeMarco said, "what's this little notation right here?"

She was pointing to the top right of the screen. A small notification gave viewers a date and time for when the files were last accessed.

"Well, that does seem a little odd, doesn't it?" Rothbridge said.

According to the database, the file on Alvin Fuller had last been accessed just eight days ago.

"Is there any way to find out who accessed it?" Kate asked.

"Sure there is," Rothbridge said. He leaned in and clicked around a bit, finally coming to the information he needed. The screen told them that an Officer Smith was the one who had accessed the Fuller file, at 3:07 p.m. eight days ago.

"Smith," Rothbridge asked. "I wonder why. Hold on, would you?"

He left the little office, closing the door behind him. Kate and DeMarco shared a confused look. Though, really, Kate was beginning to feel a stirring of excitement. If she'd felt that she had been pushed as they'd entered the police station, she now felt that they were being catapulted toward some grand revelation.

"That timing…it can't be a coincidence," Kate said.

"Yeah, doubtful," DeMarco agreed.

Something is really off here, Kate thought. Given the nature of the news they had discovered on Wendy Fuller, it opened up entire new realms of possibilities regarding Mercy. Was Mercy not even their biological child? Based on the new timelines they were looking at now, based on discovering Wendy's infertility, it certainly didn't seem like it.

Maybe they moved away from Waynesboro because they were *running from something,* Kate thought. *And maybe that something heavily involves Mercy.*

Her thoughts were interrupted when Rothbridge came back into the room. There was another officer with him, a thirty-something guy who looked very nervous. The name patch on his chest read SMITH.

"Officer Smith," Rothbridge said. "These two ladies are agents with the FBI. They're in town trying to drum up some information on Alvin and Wendy Fuller—both previous residents of Waynesboro. We looked them up in the database and saw that you had accessed their records eight days ago. Of course, that's perfectly fine. But we'd like to know *why.* Given that they were killed four days ago and their daughter is currently missing, it's interesting that you pulled up records on them prior to their murders—especially since they haven't lived in town in sixteen years."

Smith looked like he might pass out from a panic attack for a moment but then a flood of relief showed on his face. "Someone came in last week asking if we'd know how to locate a family that she thought lived here in Waynesboro," Smith said. "She said she was related. Seemed really distressed, like she had been crying. She gave me the names and I told her to wait. I came back to look it up and found out that they were apparently no longer residents."

"And how did you know that based on just these records?" DeMarco asked.

"The address is listed as Sparrow Road," Smith said.

"No one has lived on that road in over five years," Rothbridge explained to the agents.

"Officer Smith, did you get this woman's name?"

"It was Katherine. The last name I'm not sure about. Sanders? Saunders? Something like that?"

"A local?"

"No. She said she was from out of town and that the Fullers were relatives. Said she needed to speak with them about something private—something related to family issues."

"What was her reaction when you told her that they had moved?"

"She didn't seem surprised."

"Deputy Rothbridge," DeMarco said, "are there any security cameras set up in the station?"

"The only cameras we have are out in the parking lot and one in the little interrogation room we have. If this woman came in from the front, she's not going to be on any of the cameras."

"I'm sorry," Smith said. "I took down the usual information for the request. Name, reason for the information. It was quick and just sort of...I don't know. It didn't seem important."

"It's fine, Smith," Rothbridge said.

"What did she look like?" Kate asked.

"I'd say she was in her early twenties. A pretty young lady. Dark hair, sort of quiet. But she looked a little strung out. Like I said, I think she was upset about something."

"And she said she was family?"

Smith nodded, his eyes distant. He was clearly still feeling guilty about not taking down more information on this Katherine lady.

"Deputy," Kate said, "you said no one has lived out on that road for several years. If the Fullers lived there about fifteen or sixteen years ago, is there anyone who might live close enough to it that might have known the Fullers?"

"There's just no way to know."

Something then occurred to Kate. It was a long shot, but given the way the morning was going, she wasn't about to ignore *any* potential threads.

She took out her phone and pulled up the pictures she had taken from Alvin Fuller's file during their visit to Coleman Furniture and Cabinets. She found the insurance and emergency contact forms, zooming in and looking to the bottom. At the bottom of one of the personal information forms was a listing for emergency contacts, complete with addresses and phone numbers. One of those contacts was listed as Pam Crabtree of Waynesboro.

"How about this address?" Kate asked, showing the screen to Rothbridge. "Is this close?"

"It is. As a matter of fact, it's only about a mile or so away from the Fullers' old address out on Sparrow Road."

"You know if this lady still lives there?"

"She does. Her *and* her husband. The name stands out because her husband tends to raise a lot of hell at town council meetings about the lack of jobs in the area."

"Any idea if they'd be home this time of the day?"

"I can almost guarantee it. They're both retired. If memory serves, I believe Pam does alterations to clothes as a little side gig."

Kate plugged the address into her phone's GPS app as she got to her feet and instantly started for the door. "Thank you for your help," she told both of the men still standing in the records room.

"Need any assistance?" Rothbridge asked.

"I don't think so," she said.

Though, given the way the morning had gone so far, she wasn't so sure what the remainder of the day had in store.

CHAPTER TWENTY TWO

The Crabtree residence was located down a two-lane road that was bordered on both sides by towering oaks. The late morning sun pouring through, filtered through the branches and leaves, was quite beautiful. Their driveway was directly off of the road; several yards ahead, Kate could see a turn-off for the apparently now-defunct Sparrow Road.

When she pulled into the driveway, Kate parked behind one of the two vehicles already parked there: one older beat-up car and a pickup truck that, while reasonably new, had taken a beating. Kate and DeMarco walked across the yard, the quiet southern morning like some sweet music ushering them along.

Kate knocked on the door twice before it was answered. From the first knock to the moment the door was opened, roughly forty seconds had passed. The man who answered the door was tall, thin, and clearly annoyed to be receiving unexpected company.

"Yeah?" he said. "Can I help you?"

Their badges and IDs out, Kate and DeMarco introduced themselves. The man did a very poor job of hiding his alarm. And something about that alarmed expression also alarmed Kate. She again felt that sense of being pushed along, riding some track that had been built for her long ago, but unseen to her.

"We have some questions about a family that used to live in Waynesboro," Kate said. "A Pam Crabtree was listed as an emergency contact for the husband's place of employment."

The man looked trapped, like he had no idea what he should do. He opened his mouth two different times, wanting to say something but not having the words.

"Does Pam Crabtree live here?" she asked.

"Pam!" the man yelled. "There are FBI agents here to talk to you."

Kate jumped at the shouting. And she couldn't help but feel as if he had taken this approach as a way to warn her—to let her know that they had company that might cause them trouble. It made Kate feel like they might be hiding something.

"Let 'em in," a woman's voice replied from inside.

The man stepped aside and let them in. He was easily six inches taller than Kate; when they passed by him, he looked down on them like a man might observe a passing insect that had the potential to bite or sting. The front door led directly into a living room, where the man sat down carefully in an old recliner.

"What family are you trying to learn about?" he asked.

"Wendy and Alvin Fuller," Kate said. "They lived here for a while but moved about sixteen years ago. You remember them?"

The man looked confused, like he didn't understand the question. Eventually, he only shook his head.

"Are you Mrs. Crabtree's husband?" DeMarco asked.

"Yeah."

"Is she busy?"

"I don't...no, I don't think so."

"Mr. Crabtree, if you don't mind me asking, are you all right?" Kate asked. "You look very troubled about something."

"I'm fine," he said. And before he could be questioned any further, a woman came into the room from an entrance in the back of the living room. A darkened hallway sat beyond her, leading farther into the house. This woman, presumably Pam Crabtree, was just as rail thin as her husband. She looked perpetually tired and her mouth was drawn down in a sneer that made it look as if it was an expression she wore quite often.

"Alvin and Wendy Fuller?" she asked.

"Yes ma'am," Kate said. "When he was in town and working at Coleman Furniture and Cabinets, he had you listed as an emergency contact."

"Yeah, we used to be pretty close with them when they lived here. I've always had something of a problem with my right knee...have ever since I was a child. It made it damn near impossible to work, so I was living on government assistance. The Fullers came into town and when they were all moved in they came over to introduce themselves. Alvin was a nice enough fellow. Young and in love with his wife. Told me to call him whenever my knee was flaring up if I needed any help."

"And did you ever call on him?" DeMarco asked.

"Oh yeah, several times."

"Too many times," her husband replied from his place in his recliner. "He was always over here, doing things I should have been doing. He treated us like we were old and broken."

"He was a sweetie," Pam argued. "But then...he stopped coming around. He got..."

"What?" Kate asked.

"He just got mean. Like out of nowhere. And after that, I stopped calling on him for help."

"Do you recall them having a daughter?" Kate asked.

"No. No kids. Actually, I'm pretty sure they were having problems having kids. If I remember correctly, Wendy was having some tests done. But…hell, I guess that was right before they left town."

"Was there anything about them that struck you as odd?" DeMarco asked. "You said he got mean. What, exactly, do you mean?"

Before Pam could answer, another person came walking down the hallway and into the room. She was a younger woman, maybe twenty-two or twenty-three.

"It means he became an uncaring asshole," she said.

"And who are you?" Kate asked.

"I'm Katherine Sanders."

Kate and DeMarco shared an uneasy look. Just like that, a lead had literally fallen in their lap.

"The same Katherine Sanders that went by the Waynesboro police station eight days ago to ask for contact information on the Fuller family?" Kate asked.

The girl stepped into the room and sat down on the dingy couch against the back wall. She looked at both of the Crabtrees before she spoke. Kate studied the girl and within five seconds could determine that she was either high or jonesing for her next one. From the looks of the girl's lips, her frail state, and the overall tired look about her, Kate assumed meth was her drug of choice.

"Yeah. I've been trying to find them for a year or so now."

"Why is that?"

Katherine looked to Pam Crabtree, apparently expecting for some backup. Pam, though, didn't seem very comfortable with the way things were going.

"At the risk of seeming pushy," Kate said, "I'm going to need to know what in the hell is going on."

"Well," Pam said, "like the Fullers, we once knew Katherine pretty well, too. But her parents also ended up leaving town."

"Why?" DeMarco said.

"Because my father couldn't keep his stupid ass out of jail," Katherine said.

"And what's the link to the Fullers?"

"My parents and the Fullers got to know each other, I think," Katherine said. "I was young when everything happened. Like maybe five or six years old."

"What do you mean by *everything*?" Kate asked.

Katherine took a breath. She was visibly shaking—from emotion or drug withdrawal, Kate wasn't sure—and looking around the room like she was expecting someone to attack her at any moment. She finally answered, and when she did, it came out in a grumbling sort of whine, like a woman desperate to tell a secret but afraid of what it could mean.

"My dad was a criminal and my mom was a druggie," Katherine said. "But somehow, they had another baby after me. A little girl. My sister. And even though I have absolutely no proof..."

"What is it?" Kate asked, taking a step toward Katherine.

"The Fullers took her. They took my sister away and my parents never did a fucking thing about it!"

***

The atmosphere in the Crabtree living room was absolutely chilled after the comment came out of Katherine's mouth. Again, Kate and DeMarco looked uneasily at one another, shocked by the accusation.

"I'm sure you understand," Kate said, "that such an accusation is very serious. Especially when you yourself said you don't have proof."

"I know. But I remember it. Not clearly, exactly, but I do remember the Fullers being there on the day Kim was taken."

"Kim? That's your sister?"

"Yes. Kim Sanders. She couldn't have been any older than three months or so when they took her."

"How do you know they took her?" Kate asked. "Did you actually see it?"

"No. But they were there, hanging out with my parents. They were friends, I guess. I just...I remember them being there and I thought they left. I went back to my room and heard them come back. I can remember hearing some screaming later on, and then coming out. Dad was knocked out and Kim was gone."

"What did you do?"

"Well, Mom was at work when it happened. I think she had just left for her shift. So I called the Crabtrees and they came over."

Pam nodded, sitting by Katherine and taking her hand. "Katherine's parents were miserable people," she explained. "When her dad got in trouble with the police and her mother needed help caring for Katherine, she'd call us. Same with the mom. When she was too strung out to be a functioning mother and Katherine's dad couldn't handle things, he'd bring her here. We brought her here

109

that day. It was a hard decision. But I knew if we called the authorities, Katherine would end up in the foster system. And she deserved so much better than that."

"We'd keep her for days at a time sometimes," Mr. Crabtree said from his recliner. "We were happy to do it because we wanted what was best for her, but we also felt sort of stupid. We'd basically just keep her so her messed up parents could get their acts together. And really, it never happened."

"We did our best to help," Pam said. "Social Services in this part of the state is a joke. We wanted to badly to keep her out of the foster system. But I think her school caught wind of what was happening at some point…"

"Third grade," Katherine said. "My teacher somehow found out that Mom was high out of her mind when she brought me to school one morning because I missed the bus. Someone did some digging, and that was that. I bounced around the foster system for the rest of my childhood. Five different homes."

"And you never, in the course of all of that, bothered to mention that you had a sister that had been abducted?" DeMarco asked.

"No. Not too long after Kim went missing, my parents told me not to mention it. Never to mention it again. I think they were relieved. I hate to say it, I really do, but they didn't want her. Hell, half the time, I don't think they wanted me."

Kate could not get a proper read on whether Katherine's story was true or not. It didn't help that she was clearly strung out at the present moment.

"Katherine, where are your parents now?"

"Mom died ten years ago. She overdosed on heroin. Dad…" She chuckled here and gave a shrug. "I have no idea. I haven't seen or spoken to him since he reached out to me after Mom died."

"What's his name?"

"Nick. Nick Sanders."

"Are you currently using, Katherine?" Kate asked.

Katherine was apparently not expecting such a direct question. She looked nervously around the room and nodded. "Not like today. But meth. Yeah…the apple doesn't fall too far from the rotten tree, does it?"

"She came to us when she got into town," Pam explained. "We told her she could stay here for a while, but there were to be no drugs in this house."

"So why were you looking for an address for the Fullers?" Kate asked.

"Because I want to confront them. I don't care about jail time or anyone getting in trouble. I just want them to know that I know what they did. I want to meet my sister. I mean…I'm not mad at them. Hell, she probably had a better life with them than she would have if she'd stayed with my asshole parents."

Kate nearly told her about the Fullers and the missing girl that she was claiming to be her sister. But until she knew the story was factual, she wasn't going to reveal such information. But then again, she had to reveal some of it. Especially if they wanted Katherine's assistance in getting deeper into the case

"Katherine…we've been visiting Deton, Virginia, for the last few days. It's where the Fullers were living."

"Were? Did they move again?"

"No," DeMarco said. "They were murdered. Which is why we find it very interesting that you were asking about them eight days ago."

"Now wait just a minute," Pam said. "Katherine has been here with us for nearly two weeks. Ten days, I think it's been now."

Kate felt a tension headache building behind her eyes as she tried to make sense of the situation. "Katherine…would you be willing to come with us to Deton? If what you're telling us is true, you could be essential to solving the case."

"You mean figuring out who killed them?"

"That," Kate said, "and who kidnapped your sister."

Katherine seemed to fall into a slight trance at this comment. Slowly, she started to shake her head. "No. I don't want to spend any time in a police station. I can tell you everything I know and I can help over the phone or whatever, but no…I don't want to go to some other town."

Kate supposed she understood this. And really, in the grand scheme of things, it wasn't like Katherine being there in Deton would help the case move any faster.

"Katherine, what can you tell me about the Fullers? Do you remember them at all?"

"Barely. They would come over to the house every now and then, trying to be friends with my folks, I think. Over time, I started to realize that one of the reasons they never stuck around for very long was probably because of my folks' lifestyle. That and, of course, they stole my sister. She just…"

She trailed off here and looked to the ceiling. The moment a shimmer of tears started to trace the outlines of her eyes, she wiped them away. She then looked directly at Kate and despite the vague detachment in her eyes, Kate felt for her.

"Is she alive?"

"We don't know. We're trying to find her. Until this morning, we assumed she was the biological daughter of Alvin and Wendy Fuller."

For a moment, Kate thought Katherine was going to change her mind. Maybe she'd come along to Deton to help, driven by the hope of finding her long-lost sister. But again, Katherine Sanders only shook her head. She looked sad as she did so, as if she wished she were just a little braver.

If she's telling the truth, Kate thought, *this case is much bigger than we thought—and goes back much further. And perhaps even more notable...if this is a fifteen-year-old abduction case, we're soon going to run out of suspects.*

CHAPTER TWENTY THREE

While Kate made the drive from Waynesboro back to Deton, DeMarco made numerous phone calls. The result of those calls was a packed police station back in Deton. More state Police had come to assist and, almost like moths to a growing fire, there were more news vans parked outside the station.

Sheriff Barnes had apparently been waiting at the door for them because as soon as they started walking across the parking lot, swarmed by reporters and camera people, Barnes was there He stood in front of Kate and DeMarco like a moving wall, barking orders and mild threats to the reporters. Kate couldn't help but feel a little charm from the gesture.

When they were inside and away from turmoil of the press, Barnes practically collapsed in one of the chairs in the small waiting area just in front of the bullpen.

"Okay, so here's where we're at," he said. "I've got four officers, including Foster, out talking to families that had even the most remote connection to the Fullers. Many of them are repeat interviews, only this time we are asking specifically about any information they have on the Fullers' lives before moving to Deton. We're also speaking with anyone we know might have been a friend of Mercy Fuller. There are three state policemen at her high school right now, speaking with guidance counselors and teachers." He sighed here and then looked back and forth between Kate and DeMarco. "You really think this Katherine Sanders woman is telling the truth?"

"I don't know for sure," Kate said. "But I don't see why she'd have any reason to lie about it. We've got a team at the bureau working on getting current contact information on one Nick Sanders, a man who, according to Katherine, is Mercy Fuller's biological father."

"This all sounds insane to me," Barnes said.

"It's a little crazy for us as well," DeMarco said.

He led them back to the small conference room they had been using. Kate saw that several people had filled the whiteboard with names, phone numbers, dates, and other information. It looked chaotic but showed signs of a team that was very much dedicated to getting to the bottom of a case.

There was a book on the center of the table—one that Kate recognized as Mercy Fuller's journal. Barnes slapped it and slid it over to Kate.

"We've had two officers read through this, looking for anything that might indicate Mercy's knowledge of her real parents. But there's nothing. I think it's safe to say that if Wendy and Alvin Fuller *weren't* her parents, Mercy had no idea."

"It would make sense," DeMarco said. "If we're going on the assumption that Katherine Sanders is telling even a half-truth, the Fullers would have no reason to come clean."

"Sheriff Barnes, how far back can you recall the Fullers coming into town?"

"Decent, I guess. Someone moves into a town like this, it's all locals talk about for a while. I was only an officer when they arrived. Came into town with a baby in tow."

"Any idea how old Mercy would have been at that time?" Kate asked.

"Sorry, no. Surely not quite a toddler yet. Still a baby."

"I can't help but wonder if this potential abduction fifteen years ago is the motive—the reason the Fullers were killed. And if that's the case, I doubt the killer and abductor would be anyone local."

"But if Katherine Sanders has been on the hunt for her so-called sister, maybe she told other people. Maybe other family members," Barnes said.

"Based on what she told us, there would be no more family other than her father, and she claims not to have been in recent touch with him."

"Any possibility that Katherine Sanders killed them?"

"Extremely doubtful," Kate said. She looked to DeMarco to make sure she was not alone in the assumption and got a nod of agreement.

"Well, if this thing extends out to Waynesboro and Staunton, I don't know if—".

They were interrupted by a knock on the door. After Barnes yelled a quick and curt *come in,* a state trooper walked into the room. His pants were dirty around the bottom and he looked ragged and tired.

"We're going to do one last run out in Jones Field and along Blood Gulch Road," the trooper said. "But we're finding absolutely nothing. We're starting to think the abductor came in *through* Jones Field, with a car waiting along Blood Gulch Road."

"Meaning the abductor is nowhere nearby," Barnes said.

"Exactly."

This did not discourage Kate at all. She had no illusion that Mercy Fuller would be found here in Deton—if she was discovered at all.

So then where might she end up? Kate wondered.

It made her once again think about Anne Pettus, how she and Mercy were very close and would sometimes take shopping trips about an hour or so out of town. She then wondered what sorts of things Mercy did before she had friends with a driver's license. She thought about the Crabtree family and how they had cared for Katherine Sanders when her parents had been unfit.

Both Alvin and Wendy worked locally here in Deton for fifteen years, Kate thought. *Surely someone must have babysat her at some point...*

"Sheriff, in all of the records we've collected, I don't recall coming across someone that babysat Mercy when she was a child. But surely someone had to watch her after school and over the summer while her parents worked, right?"

"That's right," he said, a smile touching his lips. "There might not have been a babysitter on there because a lot of the parents take their kids to the little nursery and kids area of the Baptist church in town. It's not exactly a day care, but kind of like an unofficial preschool of sorts. And I am pretty certain the church is in the contacts..."

Kate grabbed up the file on the table, one of many copies of the Fuller files that were circulating around the station. She scanned through the names of potential people to question and came to a name with the local Baptist church—Cornerstone Baptist—written in parentheses by her name.

"Delores King," she said out loud. "You know her?"

"Oh yeah. Sweet old lady. She's somewhere in her seventies, I think. She's a permanent fixture at that church—for the little day care thing *and* on Sundays."

"You think she'd be up for a visit?"

"I can guarantee it," he said, his smile growing wider. "But be warned...be ready to have your ear talked off. That lady is the very epitome of a small-town grapevine."

This was usually a trait that unnerved Kate but given the lack of information they had to work with, she supposed a stroll through the grapevine might be exactly what they needed.

***

Barnes had been right; even give the morbid nature of their visit, Delores King seemed thrilled to have company. She had just finished handing out a snack of Goldfish crackers and apple juice to the six children she and one helper were looking after when Kate and DeMarco arrived. After Kate had explained to her why they were paying a visit, Delores led them into a small classroom near the back of the church. She smiled the entire time, though once Kate and DeMarco had shared details of the case, there seemed to be traces of sadness there, too.

The classroom Delores had brought them to was for younger children. All of the chairs were far too low to the ground, leaving the three of them to stand.

"So, as we told you," Kate said, "the church was listed as a potential child care for Mercy Fuller. Do you recall keeping her at all?"

"Yes, I do. A brilliant little girl. So brilliant, in fact, that I believe her parents allowed her to just stay at home by herself when she was ten years old or so."

"So she was here for her preschool years?" DeMarco asked.

"She was. I never truly got to know Alvin or Wendy all that well. They only ever came to church on holidays. But they always paid on time and were never late to pick up Mercy."

"Mrs. King, what I'm about to tell you is considered classified, though I doubt it will remain that way with all of the news crews around town. So I would greatly appreciate your silence on the matter. Do you understand?"

She gave a nod and Kate couldn't help but not believe her.

"Recent discoveries in the Fuller case are leading us to look into the possibility that Mercy was not the biological child of Alvin and Wendy. Were there ever any moments while she attended here where you heard Mercy say something about maybe being adopted or the Fullers not being her real parents?"

The expression on Delores's face made it clear that she had not been expecting this sort of a question. "I...well, no, nothing that I can remember. I would have never even thought of such a thing. I mean...even just looking at Mercy, she *did* bear a passing resemblance to Wendy. But nothing like Alvin...not a single feature."

"What do you remember about the Fullers when they came into town?" DeMarco asked.

"Not much, really. I thought it was weird...as did a lot of people, that a family with a brand new baby would willingly move to somewhere like Deton. Not many opportunities, you know? But

116

the little bit I knew of them....they seemed like a nice enough couple."

"Did you ever hear any gossip about them? Maybe why they came to Deton at all? Or maybe anyone that didn't really care for them?"

"No...nothing like that. I know small towns have a penchant for gossip, but Deton really isn't like that. Everyone mostly tends to get along with everyone else."

"What about Mercy herself when she was part of your preschool and childcare program?" DeMarco asked. "Was she well-behaved? Any problems with the other kids?"

"No. From what I remember, everyone liked her. She was something of a jokester, you know? Always trying to make kids laugh. A team player. I don't recall her ever throwing any tantrums or bossing the other kids around."

Kate was about to ask another question even though she was pretty sure this avenue was a dead end. Before the words could come to her, though, her cell phone rang. She gave an apologetic look to Delores, stepped outside of the room, and took the call. She was surprised to see Duran's name on the call display.

"This is Agent Wise," she said, never quite sure how to answer Duran's call now that she was in this peculiar second stage of her career.

"Wise, I thought I'd call you directly to let you know that we found the information for Nick and Helen Sanders, parents of one Katherine Sanders. Turns out Katherine was telling the truth about her mother. Helen Sanders died in an apartment in Raleigh, North Carolina, about ten years ago. Heroin overdose. As for her father...we've got an address of some place called Duck Branch, Virginia. Last known job is with a place called Bill's Tire and Auto, and that news is within at least one month of being recent."

"Where the hell is Duck Branch?"

"Looks to be about an hour and a half away from Deton. Another small backwoods sort of town."

"DeMarco and I will head down that way right now, then."

"You got enough state guys there in Deton to cover while you're gone? Do I need to send another few agents down your way?"

"I don't think so. At this point, it would just be adding to the clutter."

"Keep me posted," he said, ending the call and leaving Kate with the burdening knowledge of realizing that she and DeMarco were going to have to get back in the car and meander through the Virginia countryside yet again.

She checked the time and saw it was 3:40. She had no idea when Bill's Tire and Auto closed, but knew it would easier to meet with Nick Sanders there rather than locating his home and having an awkward meeting with him there. She ran a few scenarios through her head and then, after some quick thinking, looked up the police station nearest Duck Branch, and placed a quick call. If she was going to close this day out on a high note, it seemed she'd need all the help she could get—even if it came in the form of a small backwoods police department that had no knowledge of the recent turn of events in the Fuller case.

She wrapped the call up and reentered the room DeMarco and Delores King were still in. Delores was telling DeMarco a few details about the one time she'd had a purposeful conversation with Wendy Fuller but there was nothing of use in it.

"Mrs. King," Kate said, "thank you for your time. But we need to get going."

She hurried out of the room as politely as she could, with DeMarco falling in behind her.

"Who was on the phone?" DeMarco asked.

"We got a location on Nick Sanders. And, lucky us, it requires more driving through rural Virginia."

DeMarco said nothing, making her feelings about more car riding unclear. But the one thing Kate *did* see in DeMarco was an unwavering determination. In the steely expression DeMarco wore, Kate could see the foundations of a woman who was going to become an incredible agent, living out a grand career. But more important, she also saw the spark of a woman who was not going to rest until this case was solved. And there was no way a seemingly endless stream of Virginia back roads was going to derail her.

Kate could relate. It was exactly how she felt as she pulled her car back out onto the thin strip of road that would lead back to Highway 44 and the winding, waiting roads beyond.

CHAPTER TWENTY FOUR

All of the rural Virginia back roads looked the same as far as Kate was concerned. Blacktop—some unmarked with signs or lines down the middle—and expanses of woodlands that were slowly being decimated by local lumber companies. Over and over again. And Duck Branch was no different. It was a little hole in the wall town, nearly every business closed up like the echo of some better life from a decade or so ago.

About halfway through the sorry excuse for a town, Bill's Tire and Auto Shop came up on the right. There wasn't even any real sign out front—just an old piece of double-enforced plywood with the name of the business painted on in black. It was 5:25 when Kate pulled her car into the bumpy parking lot. There were several old beaten-up vehicles parked along the side of the building, clearly in need of repair. The only other two vehicles to be seen were a run-down old Ford truck and a police car with *Carroll County Sheriff* written down the side.

It was the Carroll County police that Kate had spoken to in Cornerstone Baptist Church after getting off of the phone with Duran. She'd called in an assist for an officer to detain Nick Sanders until she and DeMarco could arrive, and the fellow on the line had seemed pleased to help.

Kate and DeMarco got out of the car and walked over to the patrol car. A short and slightly overweight man got out, adjusting his pants as he walked toward them. Kate was rather ashamed of herself when she thought he looked like the stereotypical southern cop—pretty much like something straight out of *The Dukes of Hazard.*

Because the cop was scrutinizing them so heavily as they approached one another, Kate went ahead and pulled her badge and ID. The cop nodded and extended a meaty hand to be shaken.

"I'm Sheriff Jennings," he said. "I got your boy Nick Sanders in the front seat of my car and let me tell you, he's pretty pissed."

"Did you arrest him?" Kate asked.

"Nope. Nothing to arrest him for. But I did tell him I had some specialist coming in to speak to him. Told him if he hung out here with me until you got here, it would make things much easier. I tell you, though...I have a mind to arrest him anyway. He's being

119

difficult about answering questions. When I told him I'd like to see his cell phone, he got mad. I thought I was going to have a fight on my hands. He's demanding a warrant before we can get his phone."

"Did you make a call for that?"

"Sure did. I expect to have it in an hour or so. The phone is in his truck," Jennings said, gesturing toward the beat-up truck beside his patrol car.

"You mind if we speak to him?" Kate asked.

"That's fine. But…can I ask what this is about?"

"He's a suspect for two murders and a possible abduction up in Deton," Kate said. "And there may be unlikely ties to the victims. That's all I can say for now."

"Can't say I'm surprised," Jennings said. "This guy has been nothing but trouble since he moved to town."

"How long has he been here?" DeMarco asked.

"Four or five years, I'd guess. Came here from Richmond after a shit load of legal issues. Truth be told, if you can get him out of town, I'd consider it a favor."

He walked to the passenger side of the patrol car and opened the door. "Get on out here, Sanders," Jennings said. "These two ladies would like to speak with you."

The man who emerged from the police cruiser bore an uncanny resemblance to Katherine Sanders. He was rail-thin, had a haunted distant look in his eyes, and, as Jennings had said, he looked incredibly angry. He had long hair that looked as if it had not been washed in a few days. He also had that same hazy faraway look she had seen in Katherine's eyes.

Again, Kate and DeMarco showed their ID and badges. Seeing them, Nick Sanders looked instantly alarmed. It was another moment where he looked exactly like his older daughter.

"Mr. Sanders, we're currently investigating a case in Deton, Virginia, that seems to have a direct link to you. Do you recall the Fuller family from your time in the Waynesboro?"

The alarm on his face now turned to something that resembled genuine fear. Kate thought it was the look of a man who was having his mind read. He felt like his own thoughts and memories were being intruded upon.

"I do."

"When was the last time you saw the Fullers?"

"A long time ago."

"Would you be at all surprised to know that both Alvin and Wendy Fuller are dead?"

The news seemed to rock him but he took it in stride. He looked from Jennings and then to the two women standing in front of him. "Who killed them?"

"We don't know yet," Kate said. "And honestly, we thought you might be a little concerned about what had become of their fifteen-year-old daughter."

For just a moment, Nick Sanders looked like someone had slapped him. He recoiled just a bit, his mouth dropping slightly open.

"We spoke to your daughter earlier today," Kate said. "Katherine. She was in Waynesboro. Apparently, she was searching for the address of Wendy and Alvin Fuller. Do you have any idea why that might be?"

Still, Nick said nothing. He looked paralyzed and out of sorts. Kate also noticed that his hands were trembling. There was a slight tic at the corner of his mouth, too. While these weren't telltale signs of meth use, they were indicators. She suddenly felt very bad for Katherine Sanders, realizing the influences she had grown up with.

"Mr. Sanders," Jennings said, "I suggest you say something."

"Like what?" he said, staring at the agents. "You know, right? You know what happened with me, my wife, and the Fullers? Is that why you're here? The Fullers are dead...so what about Kim? Is she dead, too?"

The name Kim did not register with Kate at first, but then she remembered Katherine telling them that her sister's name had been Kim. Before the Fullers had taken her, Mercy Fuller's name had been Kim Sanders.

"We don't know," Kate said. "There's currently a manhunt underway for her."

"And given that," DeMarco said, "we need to ask you about where you've been the last several days."

The reality of what DeMarco was suggesting slowly dawned on him. He chuckled, but it was an evil sound, one that was suppressed by a sneer. "Are you fucking kidding me?" he asked.

"Watch your mouth," Jennings said.

"Mr. Sanders, the sheriff tells us you won't let him look at your phone. Why is that?"

"Because it's my phone. There's private stuff on there."

"Like what?"

Again, he only sneered. He looked at the three people standing before him, studying them. Kate was fully expecting him to break off into a run at any moment.

"There's a warrant coming," Jennings said. "All you're doing is buying about an hour or so."

"And pissing us off," DeMarco said.

Kate couldn't be sure, but she thought she could see the traces of tears in Sanders' eyes. Slowly, almost as if he were mocking them, he held his hands out to them, wrists up.

"Arrest me, if you think you need to," he said.

"Do we need to?"

He smirked, but it was clear that he was nervous. He knew he was trapped and that there was trouble coming. "My phone is on the dashboard of my truck."

Kate walked over to the truck and opened the door. The inside smelled of grime, sweat, and stale cigarette smoke. She saw the cell phone sitting on the dashboard along with a few old pieces of mail and Burger King receipts. She took it out and found, without much surprise, that it was locked.

"What's the passcode?" she asked.

"One, seven six, two," he said. He spoke slowly, again making it feel like he was mocking them. He was essentially giving up, but he was finding a way to be difficult about it.

Kate unlocked the phone. She went to photos and found nothing of interest at all. Just a few photos of old trucks and truck parts. She then checked the text messages and found only a handful. Most were to people looking for freelance engine repair. Another was from a woman Nick was apparently in a sexual relationship with.

She then checked recent calls and it was there that she stopped. She didn't even have to scroll before she saw something that stuck out. There was a number he had called twice in the last three days. And it had an area code shared with Deton—a different area code than she had seen for Carroll County when she had called the police earlier.

Kate called the number, her eyes locked on Nick Sanders. DeMarco had not cuffed him, but he still held his hands out as if he were waiting for it to be done at any moment.

In Kate's ear, the phone went directly to voicemail.

The voice she heard in the recorded message made her blood feel as if it had been injected with ice water.

"Hey, guys, this is Mercy. Leave a message at the beep."

CHAPTER TWENTY FIVE

Kate almost hated to admit it, but she was glad there was just her and DeMarco to question Nick Sanders. Sure, Barnes, Foster, and all of his men had been an immense help to this point. But with them there had also been the buzzing of reporters outside and that small-town sense of community where people refused to believe that something so bad could happen in their town. She thought fondly of Barnes as she and DeMarco were led through the Carroll County police station; it was even smaller than the one in Deton, though it had been newly renovated, and the rooms were a little more spacious.

That included the interrogation room Nick Sanders was placed in. Kate stood outside of the room as Jennings and two officers carted Nick Sanders inside, cuffing him to the table and reading him his rights.

DeMarco watched through the partially open door and spoke to Kate under her breath. "I know this may seem like an unprofessional question," she said. "But what in the hell is going on here?"

"I've got theories, but they all seem a little nuts," Kate said.

"Have you ever seen anything like this?"

"No," Kate answered honestly. "No, I haven't."

Sheriff Jennings came out of the room, flanked by the two officers that had been assisting. "He's all yours," he said. "Want me to call Deton and fill them in on what's going on?"

"That would be perfect," Kate said. "And thank you for your help."

"While you're at it," DeMarco added, "could we get his record when you get a chance?"

Jennings nodded to one of the officers beside him and they went elsewhere right away to get the records. The sheriff then left Kate and DeMarco to their business with one final look back into the interrogation room.

They walked into the room slowly, almost casually. DeMarco closed the door behind them and leaned slightly against the back wall as Kate took the one seat on the side of the table opposite Sanders.

"When was the last time you saw the daughter you named Kim?" Kate asked. "The daughter that, for the last fifteen years, was known as Mercy Fuller?"

"I haven't seen her since the day the Fullers took her."

"You need to walk us through that," Kate said. "Because anyone in their right mind would expect that you'd call the police to report a kidnapping. Did you *ever* report an abduction?"

"No," he said. He would not look at either of them and his voice was trembling...not quite on the brink of tears but clearly wrestling with some sort of unexplored emotion. It was clear he was ashamed of the choices he and his wife had made.

"And why not?" DeMarco asked.

"Because we were assholes. We were selfish. Kim...we didn't plan for her. We didn't want another baby. Shit...we were pretty sure the hospital would keep her. We were sure she'd be born with something in her system. Not that we were trying to kill the baby or anything; we weren't *that* messed up."

"What about Katherine?" Kate asked. "Was she a planned pregnancy?"

"Yeah. Me and Helen tried having a baby right after we got married."

"Were you using then?"

"Pot here and there. Coke once or twice. But the meth and the heroin didn't come until a few years later."

"Tell us how you got to know the Fullers."

"I don't remember how we met them. For real. I think maybe it was at a bar or something. We got along with them. We ended up hanging out a lot. Just to get together to drink, you know? I think we sort of scared them off when we got into the heavy stuff. I mean...when Helen started heroin...that was it. That was the end of her. And we knew we were shit parents. We were just lucky no one ever stepped in, you know? Like social services or whatever. We were really lucky."

"Tell me about the day you and Katherine claim the Fullers took Kim from you," Kate said.

"It was a Sunday. I know because we had asked them to come over to watch the Redskins play. They were playing the Cowboys— and the Fullers liked the Cowboys. We were surprised when they actually agreed. They had been sketchy around us, sort of distancing themselves from us. I figured it was because of the coke and her heroin. I felt like they were sort of starting to look down on us."

"So they came over. And was there a fight?"

"No. Helen was working as a waitress. She got called in for an emergency shift. Someone got sick or something. It's been what, fifteen years…I don't remember all of it. But she had to leave and work…we couldn't turn down any shifts, you know? Needed the money. Anyway…she's gone for like maybe half an hour and then Alvin and Wendy say they need to get going. They left, you know…and I just sat there and watched the game with little Katherine. Kim was in her little crib thing. She was like maybe three months old. But then there's a knock on the door. I got up and answered it and it's Alvin. Before he punched me the first time, I saw that he was crying…like messed up about something, you know?"

"So they left and came back?" DeMarco asked.

"Yeah…pretty sure that's how it happened. The first punch broke my nose. I swung back at him but missed. And then he just sort of laid into me. I remember two or three more punches and then I was out. Blacked out. It was Katherine that got me to come back around. She was in another room when Alvin came back…she was calling me and trying to get me to sit up. She said Kim was missing."

"And you weren't scared or upset about that?" Kate asked.

"Of course I was. I called Helen and then…I was going to call the police but we had drugs in the house. Helen had shot up that morning. It was too risky. And the more we talked about it, the more we thought about it…we just decided maybe Kim was better off. Maybe *we* were better off…"

Nick did start weeping this time. It was as if the weight and tragedy of the decision to simply not report the abduction of their child fifteen years ago came crashing down on him in that moment. It came out in hitching sobs that Kate allowed him to get out before forging on.

"Mr. Sanders, how did you come to have Mercy's number?"

"I started looking for her about six months ago. Or, I guess I started trying to find the Fullers. Katherine had found me and asked where Kim was. She found it hard to believe the story…that we just let her go."

"Katherine didn't stay with you long either, right? She ended up in foster care."

"Look, I don't need you reminding me how much of a terrible parent I was. I fucked up. I was stupid and selfish. I'm still all those things. But a man can only live with regret so long."

A knock at the door silenced him. Sheriff Jennings stepped in, quickly handed Kate a thick folder and headed back out. Kate opened it up and saw Nick's criminal record. There were several entries, most of them distributing and manufacturing crystal meth. There were also a few for assault and battery. He'd never stayed in jail for more than two months at a time, but the records went back almost twenty years—long before his second daughter had been born.

"When did you and your wife leave Waynesboro?" Kate asked.

"Not too long after Kim got taken. Helen started hitting the drugs harder then. She didn't want Kim back but she was mad at herself because of it, you know? She stiffed a few dealers, so we hit the road. Never really stayed in one place or very long. I've been in Duck Branch for about four years now and that's the longest I've stayed put since we left Waynesboro."

"We're going to need to know where you were every night for the past week or so," Kate said. "Are you prepared to give us those answers?"

"I was around, you know? Out drinking, just doing my thing, you know?"

"No. I don't know. I'd also like to know how you got Mercy Fuller's phone number."

"I paid this private eye. A guy up in Lynchburg."

"What's his name?" DeMarco asked.

"I can't tell you that. He asked me not to tell people he was getting involved."

"Mr. Sanders," Kate said, doing her best to keep her anger in check. "Based on this folder I now have in my hands, I have no reason to believe you. And quite frankly, until you come clean and tell me where you've been the last few nights or supply me with the real source of Mercy Fuller's phone number, you *will* remain under arrest for the murder of Alvin and Wendy Fuller as well as the abduction of Mercy Fuller."

"How the hell do you abduct something that was yours in the first place?" he spat.

"Why don't you tell me?" Kate said.

Her rage was growing quickly. She needed a break. The more certain she became that Nick Sanders had something to do with the Fuller case, the more she wanted to lash out at him. How could he be so flippant about the welfare of both of his daughters? She had seen negligent parenting in her line of work before, sure, but this was taking things to an entirely different level.

She left the room, headed straight through the station, and to the parking lot. Night had fallen about an hour ago. She looked up to the night sky, alive and vibrant with stars and the absence of light pollution she was used to in Richmond. She thought of Melissa and Michelle, not too far away under these same stars. She wanted nothing more than to hold little Michelle in that moment. She wanted it so badly that it brought tears to her eyes. She clenched her fists, trying to recall a time a suspect had angered her so badly.

"I see he was getting to you, too."

DeMarco's voice broke through the quiet of the night. Kate turned to face her, not caring if the wetness of the tears in her eyes was giving her away.

"He was," Kate admitted. "And he's guilty of something. I don't know if it's the Fuller murders or not, but he's not coming clean about something. He knows more than he's letting on."

"We can call the state guys up in Deton," DeMarco said. "Have them come get him and take him to Richmond."

"I think that's our best bet. Until he can give us some solid answers, he's definitely the most solid suspect we've had to this point."

"You buy the bullshit about the PI?"

"Not one bit. And it's also weird that he's not even *trying* to come up with an alibi for the past few nights. No lies, no stories, nothing."

DeMarco nodded at this as she, too, started to look skyward. She sighed and then looked to Kate with the most sincerity Kate had ever seen out of her.

"You're an amazing agent and likely the strongest woman I know," DeMarco said. "But you should be home with your daughter and granddaughter. In light of what they've been through, you're wasting your time and your passion on trying to figure out men like Nick Sanders."

"You're right," she said. "But one thing Melissa knows about me—and hopefully something Michelle will come to understand—is that I have to stand up for those that can't stand up for themselves. And right now, God help her, that person is Mercy Fuller. I can't go back home until we find her."

"No matter what?" DeMarco asked.

"Dead or alive, no matter what," Kate said.

The comment drifted into the night and the stars twinkled overhead as if burdened by the weight of it.

CHAPTER TWENTY SIX

The crackers were gone and she hadn't had water in about a day. She guessed it was a day. She wasn't sure. She couldn't tell the passage of time in this dark place. She had come to the conclusion that she was indeed in some sort of trailer. Not a big one like the ones on the back of big rigs, but maybe one like the smaller U-Hauls or those PODs storage units.

She also figured she'd been here for at least three days. She had her own clock worked out in her head. The times he came and spoke to her, it was probably sometime during the day—during the waking hours. Then, later, there would be the sounds of crickets and tree frogs and the world would go quiet. That was the night. And she had experienced three of them.

Now, though, she assumed it was the day. She could hear his footfalls. He was coming back to speak with her. Every time she had heard him walking, it was followed by his tapping on the outside of the container and speaking with her.

"Thirsty?"

She had been expecting his voice but even then, it chilled her. It made her want to start crying. She was not a stupid girl. He was keeping her for some damned reason. To rape her or abuse her or kill her. None of those options were great ones and she did not want to find out what he had in mind.

"I'm going to let you out," he said. "You and I, we need to figure out what we're going to do—where we go from here. I might…well, I might ask you to do some things to me. I don't know yet. But I'm not a savage. I'm not going to keep you in there, in that dark place. So I'm going to open this door and you and I are going into my house. I'll give you some of the cornbread I have left over from dinner. I have some Cokes in there, too. Beer, too…but I guess you're too young for that. So…yeah. I'm going to open this thing up. You try to run, I *will* catch you. And I *will* kill you. I have a rifle right here in my hand and I'll use it. Do you believe me?"

The mere idea of being out of the dark was enough to make her answer. The rifle did not bother her. Hell, in that moment, any crude and psycho things he wanted her to do to him didn't bother her. She just wanted out of the darkness.

She listened to keys jangling and then something heavy making a *clunk* sound. And then, holy of holies, there was light. Not a lot of it, but it was more than the absolute darkness she had been living inside for the last several days. Wherever she was, it was night. The air was relatively cool and smelled musty—not too dissimilar from the smell of the trailer she'd been in.

"You can come out," his voice said.

She had been so distracted by that fake sense of freedom that she had not realized that she was about to see his face. She had only heard his voice so far. And she'd felt his punch. A hard one, right to her face. Her lips had busted and she'd bitten down on her tongue. There had been so much blood from that little attack, she was convinced that it was the sight and the taste of her own blood that had caused her to black out and not the punch itself.

She stepped out of the trailer, taking a small step down from where the lip of the back opened up about a foot off of the ground.

"Do you want some food?" he asked.

She nodded, but could not stop herself from asking the first question out of her mouth. "Are you going to kill me?"

He laughed, but there was no humor in it. "God no. That would be stupid. That would be a waste. No…you and I are going to be on the move soon, I think. And I need you to trust me."

"Might have been a better start to that by not kidnapping me. And killing my parents."

He nodded, his face barely illuminated from a single overhead bulb behind him. He looked to be about fifty or so. He had black hair, a black beard, and hollow eyes. "You've got some spunk," he said. "I like that. You're going to be fun. Now…come on. Let's get you some food and water."

He turned and started walking. She thought about trying to knock him down and run away. But he was holding that rifle in his left hand. It looked familiar. It looked…

It was my dad's, she thought. *He killed them with the rifle and then stole it.*

Again, she recalled hearing the gunshots. Right after her father told her to run…

Her thoughts were interrupted by several rampaging thoughts. *You've been through a pretty severe trauma. Can you remember anything else about the night he took you? Anything that will help you get free? You were barely aware enough to take off your jacket in the field… You've been through the wringer, kid.*

She looked at the rifle and figured for now it might just be better to do what he said. Besides…she had dropped her jacket in the field as she had come in and out of her haze. Maybe someone had found it. Maybe the cops were looking for her. Maybe...

She stepped forward, looking around and trying to make sense of where she was. It was an old barn or shed of some kind—a floor made of wooden boards under her feet. Her steps made hollow sounds, making her think there was another floor under her, a cellar perhaps. Other than the trailer (which, she saw, was indeed some sort of old moving trailer that went on the back of a truck), the barn seemed to be mostly empty. There were rotted hay bales pressed against the far wall and what looked to be an old workbench of some kind, but other than that the place was empty.

He was waiting for her at the door, standing patiently. As she neared him, she started to tremble. She tried passing by him quickly, just to be out of his presence. When she did, he reached out and took her arm. His touch was gentle but made her cringe.

"You don't have to be afraid of me," he said. "I'm not going to kill you."

"What are you going to do to me?" she asked. She feared the answer but figured it would be better to know rather than to have that fear of the unknown in her head.

"I don't know just yet," he said.

It was not the answer Mercy had been hoping for. In fact, it somehow felt like the worst possible answer he could have given.

CHAPTER TWENTY SEVEN

By the time the state police had come down from Deton and taken Nick Sanders into custody, Kate could feel the toll of the day wearing on her. Nick had refused to give any information as to his whereabouts over the last few nights and he would not come off of the information regarding how he'd gotten Mercy Fuller's phone number. It felt almost too easy, but Kate was starting to think that maybe he was the killer and potential abductor.

But her instincts did not seem pleased with this. Even as she and DeMarco watched the trooper pull the patrol car out of the Carroll County police station parking lot, Kate felt that they were missing something.

"Something's bothering you," DeMarco pointed out.

"You're getting too good at reading me. Stop it."

DeMarco smiled. "It feels right, I think. You know, he's under arrest of suspicion of murder and child endangerment, possible kidnapping. We have every right to check out his house."

"I think that's a good idea," Kate said. "Because honestly, you're right. It feels right. All the pieces fit and Nick Sanders is definitely the sort of guy that might be capable of something like this. But his unanswered questions are big ones. And it makes me feel like we're missing something."

"You look tired," DeMarco said. "Pull up his address, and I'll do the driving."

They piled into their car as Kate plugged Nick Sanders' address into the map app on her phone. As she did so, she saw that it was 10:09; the night seemed as if it had settled on the little town ages ago, making the day seem even longer.

Fortunately, Duck Branch, much like Deton, was incredibly small. They made the trip down a series of back roads from the Carroll County police station to Nick's residence in under twenty minutes. He lived in a trailer park that housed eight mobile homes, all of which looked like they were just one wind storm away from being relocated. DeMarco located Nick's trailer and parked in the small square of dirt that served as his driveway.

As they got out of the car, Kate could hear the thumping bass of rap music coming from elsewhere in the park. Somewhere else, an infant was screaming. And it all seemed to bounce from the trees and countryside, as if there were no escape from any of it.

There was no porch on Nick's house...just a set of wide concrete stairs that led up to the front door. It was made to look like woods but Kate was pretty sure it was about as thin and hollow as an ice cream cone. She tried the door and found it locked. Undaunted, she reached into the inner pocket of her jacket, where she had been keeping a small lock-pick set for the last thirty years of her life. As she set to work on Nick Sanders' front door, Kate estimated that she had used this kit at least fifty times over the span of her career. She enjoyed the feel of DeMarco watching with a reserved kind of respect and awe.

The lock popped easily, and Kate opened the door right away. They were met at once by the overwhelming stench of cigarette smoke and what smelled like old frying grease. Kate found a light switch along the edge of the doorframe and flipped it on. The light revealed a cluttered mess of a trailer. The living room and kitchen were all connected, separated by only a thin bar area that was littered with old paper plates, empty beer cans, and strewn mail.

The living room contained an old recliner, a scarred coffee table, and a flat-screen TV that was propped up on an old bookcase against the far wall. A few sets of dirty clothes were scattered on the floor.

Kate and DeMarco gave one another of nod of acknowledgment, an unspoken sign that they would split up and search the house. Given the size and the lack of any sort of cleanliness or organization, it was not a task that Kate expected to take very long. DeMarco headed left, into the kitchen and the thin hallway beyond it. Kate turned to the living room and the single room that sat to the far side of it. The doorway opened to reveal the edge of a bed and more dirty clothes.

Kate had investigated places much worse than this one—places rife with cockroaches, mold, mildew, blood, and unnamable sticky substances on the floor. Still, the idea that this could potentially be the home of a man who had not only willingly abandoned a child fifteen years ago but was not capable of murder to get her back...well, it was a little unnerving.

But the more she searched, the less certain she became that Nick Sanders was the killer. She had no idea why he was refusing to tell them where he had been the last few nights. Much of the garage and debris around the house told some of the story: he had been here most of the time, eating frozen dinners and, according to the empty pizza box stashed beneath the coffee table and the hardened crust inside, ordering a pizza within the last three days or so.

When she got to the bedroom, she thought she understood why he was being so secretive, though. While the bedroom was slightly cleaner than the living room, there was still lots of evidence as to how he spent his time. The room smelled of body odor and burnt matches. An ashtray sat on the bedside table, badly needing to be dumped. The table was the sort that had a single drawer built into it. It was partially open, having been closed in haste the last time it had been used. Kate opened it up and saw more than enough reason for a man like Nick Sanders to remain quiet about what he had been up to the last few nights.

There were two baggies and three pill bottles in the drawer. The baggies contained about an ounce of crystal meth each. Two of the pill bottles held cocaine, and the third contained some sort of pills. It wasn't ecstasy from what she could tell. Probably some kind of speed or other methamphetamine if she had to guess.

As she closed the drawer, she saw a little lock box stashed under the bed, one of the corners sticking out. She did not like the idea of sitting on Sanders' nasty floor, so she picked the lock box up and placed it on the bedside table. She used her lock-pick set once more to pop the lid of the box open.

There were two rolls of cash inside, held together by rubber bands. She flipped through them and found about twelve thousand dollars...probably from selling drugs. There was also a St. Christopher medallion in the box, along with another baggie of a powder-like substance that looked to have once been in crystalized form—not meth, but something else.

DeMarco poked her head in the room, looked around, and wrinkled her nose. "Find anything?" she asked.

"A nice little assortment of drugs," she answered. "Probably enough for him to not want to let us know what he'd been up to the last few nights. You?"

"Just an old storage room, a bathroom, and the laundry room. Nothing out of the ordinary except an enormous stack of pornography."

"I'm pretty sure he's selling, too," Kate said. "There's twelve grand here, with meth, coke, and what I think might be DMT."

"But no evidence to support a trip to Deton or where he might have gotten Mercy's phone number?"

"No. Nothing like that. We could get forensics to check all of these dirty clothes but other than that, I don't see much of anything here for us."

133

"Same here," DeMarco said. "I think we find some place to sleep for the night and maybe try his boss over at Bill's Tire and Auto in the morning."

The idea of sleep was enticing. Kate wasn't sure when she'd last had a day feel as if it had dragged on this long. She looked to her phone and saw that it was 11:02—probably too late to call to check up on Melissa.

"Now we just need to figure out this one last mystery before ending the night," Kate said.

"What mystery?"

"Where the hell is the closest motel in a place like this?"

***

As it turned out, they had to drive nearly half an hour to find the nearest motel. It was a privately owned place, run by a married couple, two towns over. It was actually closer to the Carroll County police station than it was to Nick Sanders' trailer.

When Kate woke up the following morning, she felt refreshed and invigorated despite only getting six hours of sleep the night before. When she woke up by her own internal alarm at 5:55, she felt rather proud of herself. But then she saw the little note sitting on DeMarco's bed. It read: *Left at 5:30. There's a McDonald's down the road. Need coffee. I'll bring back breakfast.*

Kate had grabbed a shower last night, so it didn't take her very long to get ready for the day. She had the urge to go for a quick run, feeling restless and anxious to get the day started. She assumed they'd head back to Deton after speaking with Bill of Bill's Tire and Auto. With Nick Sanders in custody in Richmond and no real leads sitting elsewhere, she actually thought they might end up in Richmond before the day was over with. And that suited her just fine; maybe she'd be able to sneak in a quick trip to visit Melissa to see how they were doing.

DeMarco arrived ten minutes later with breakfast and coffee. Kate found herself ravenous, realizing that she had somehow skipped dinner yesterday. It wasn't much of a breakfast but with a sausage biscuit and hash browns in her stomach, she and DeMarco headed back out toward Duck Branch with coffees in hand.

When they arrived at Bill's Tire and Auto at 8:01, there was only one customer. A lone man—presumably Bill—was taking a tire off of a newer model van. The owner stood to the side, kicking absently at a stray bit of trash in the parking lot.

Kate was all about safety first so she waited for Bill to completely remove the tire before she approached him. He was in a small garage, and there was a small shop of sorts attached to the small office and shop building. He looked up to them and sighed.

"You the agents?" he asked.

"We are," Kate said. "Agents Wise and DeMarco."

"You the reason I don't have anyone to help today, then?" Apparently, he was not impressed with their professional approach or their accolades.

Kate looked over to the owner of the van, his eyes locked on the two strange women. "Could you please excuse us?" she asked him. "We'd like to speak in private."

The owner of the van frowned but gave a nod. He then walked into the little office that was attached to the garage. Kate watched him through the large window as he started to look at the small rack of snack crackers on the counter.

"I take it you're Bill?" Kate asked.

"I am. Can I ask why you're here?"

"We were hoping you could give us some more information about Nick Sanders. He's not exactly being very forthcoming with certain details of his life."

"He in bad trouble? Is it drugs?"

"He's in trouble one way or the other," Kate said. "We are still trying to get a clear picture of what sort of trouble, though."

"Well, he's always been in some kind of trouble," Bill said. He was rolling a new tire out and positioning it on the now-vacant wheel well on the van. "What do you need to know?"

"Did you ever hear him talk about his family?" DeMarco asked.

"A few times. But just passing stuff. I know his wife died. He never said as much but I figured if she was like him, it was probably drugs. Said he had a daughter that he hadn't seen in several years."

"Just one daughter?"

"Yeah, I think so."

"You ever get any trouble out of him?" Kate asked.

"Nothing bad. He' come in late a lot of the time but I'd just take it from his pay. When he put his mind to it, he was a hard worker. Sometimes when I have to work Saturdays I'd call him in and he was always happy to make the extra money, you know? He'd come in drunk or high sometimes and I'd chew his ass about it but that was about it."

"Any cross words between you other than that?"

"None that I can think of. I knew he was all messed up. I knew it when he came into Duck Branch four or five years ago. But I'm all about helping folks that want to help themselves, you know? I had an open spot, he was fully capable of the work, so I hired him. Some of the other guys I had working for me at the time didn't like him, though."

"Why was that?" Kate asked.

"Nick was a smart ass. You could never correct him on anything. Always wanted to argue. Hell, just two months ago he and my other worker got into a fight. Like an actual fist fight. I sent them both home and would have fired them on the spot if I didn't need the help."

"Do you know what the fight was about?"

"No," Bill said. But I figured it was a woman. I kept hearing them mention *she* and *her*."

"Is this other worker coming in today?"

"No. He quit last month. Got a job at that custom body paint place in Wells."

"Wells?" Kate asked.

"Yeah, one of the only towns in Carroll County that are managing to hang on. He left me so that left just Nick. And now I guess he's gone, too. I got to get that friggin' help wanted sign back out, I suppose."

"Could we have a name and address for this man?" DeMarco asked.

"His name is Jack Kramer. I don't have an exact address for you, but he lives on Old Acre Road. Turn off of Highway 51 and his is the fifth house you'll come to...the last one on that road before the dirt road takes over."

"Thank you," Kate said. She and DeMarco turned away, headed back for their car. Before they made it, though, Bill's voice stopped them.

"You asked about another kid...if Nick had one," he said. "He only ever mentioned one kid—a daughter. And he rarely mentioned his wife. But...well, whenever he did mention either of them, I always thought he looked sad as hell. Like he regretted what had happened. More than just losing a wife, but something else. Something he never talked about. I don't know if that helps you or not."

Kate considered it for a moment. She nodded her thanks as they got into the car, wondering if maybe Nick Sanders had lived the last fifteen years with a knot of regret in his stomach...if beyond all of the drugs and bad life decisions there had been a little seed of paternal love buried down beneath it all.

As they pulled out of the parking lot, DeMarco's phone rang. Kate listened to the one side of the conversation as she did her best to remember where, exactly, Highway 57 came in on the stretch of road they were currently on. Again, all of these damned country roads were starting to look the same.

DeMarco's side of the conversation was rather uneventful. Kate got the impression that she was speaking to someone in authority. There were a string of *Yes sir* and *I understand*. There was also a very brief rundown on the morning's plan of attack, including their current outing to find the home of Jack Kramer. The conversation lasted less than three minutes. When she ended the call, DeMarco sighed and looked over at Kate.

"I need you to head back to the motel. Director Duran wants one of us on a conference call with the state PD and Barnes. It seems Nick Sanders is still not talking. Until we can make it to Richmond, Skyping in is going to be the best we can do. He also wants us up in Richmond by the end of the day to take over the interrogation."

"What about Jack Kramer?"

"Duran says one of us can stay on the case. Only one of us needs to call in."

"Not it," Kate quipped with a sarcastic smile.

"Hey, I'm good with that. I've had my fill of the local flavor. I'll take stuffy Skype calls over trailers like Nick Sanders's any day."

Kate felt that she might be wasting her time going to speak with Jack Kramer. Just based on what she had seen of Nick Sanders (and the many details in his police record), Kate didn't find it hard at all to believe that someone might want to smash his face in. Still, there was the small chance that perhaps Jack Kramer had some insights into Nick's personal life. And if there even juts a scant few, it might be worth the trip. It would perhaps even give them some ammunition for the next time they spoke with Nick Sanders—ammunition he might not expect them to have.

The important thing was that she was starting to feel good about the case. They were definitely heading somewhere, and she didn't think one more stop by a local's home would derail them at all.

Besides, it was still early. Depending on the length of DeMarco's Skype call, she figured they could be in Richmond by noon. And if Kate could be in the same city where their likely guilty part was currently being housed *and* where her daughter was wrestling with having just dodged a scary situation, Kate would consider that a win.

CHAPTER TWENTY EIGHT

Kate was fully expecting no one to be home. She arrived at Jack Kramer's house at 8:40, figuring he was probably at work—at the body detail shop that Bill of Bill's Tire had seemed to scoff at. But when she pulled into the small gravel driveway, she saw a single truck parked in the driveway. The house itself was rustic and simple and, like a lot of the trailers tucked just off of the back roads, looked like it was just a few years from falling in on itself.

The lawn looked as if it had been freshly cut and that was about the only positive thing she could say about the property. Out to the back, the yard stopped suddenly, overtaken by weeds for several yards before the forest took over. An old doghouse sat to the side of the yard, along with what looked like a few old lengths of copper wire.

Kate walked up onto the thin porch. The wood was partially dry rotted. A wasp nest clung to the far corner, thankfully quiet. Kate knocked on the door and it sounded like the door was just as weak and rotted as some of the boards of the porch.

She heard footfalls approaching quickly—so quickly that she could feel the reverberations through the old porch boards. The door opened about halfway, a man of about forty or so peering out at her. He wore no shirt and his hair was wet, indicating that he had just gotten out of the shower. He looked perplexed to see a woman standing there in front of him—and even more off his game when she showed him her identification.

"I'm Agent Kate Wise, FBI," she said. "I'm in town investigating a man that I'm told you recently had a physical altercation with."

His eyes suddenly seemed to focus and his posture relaxed a bit. "Nick Sanders?" he asked.

"That's the one."

"Doesn't surprise me. That asshole is a mess. And believe me…I'll tell you everything you want to know."

"Do you have a few minutes?"

"Sure. I don't have to clock in until ten."

He opened the door the rest of the way but made sure to always have his eyes on her when she entered. He simply stared at her for a moment as she stepped through the doorway and into the living room. After an awkward silence, he seemed to realize for the first time that he didn't have a shirt on.

"Let me grab a shirt," he said, hurrying off through the living room elsewhere into the house.

Kate used the opportunity to look around the living room, trying to get a better gauge on the sort of man Jack Kramer might be. He had an older model television sitting on an entertainment center that had seen better years. There were a few DVDs scattered around it, mostly action titles. The house had the smell of a place that had not seen a good cleaning in a while but there wasn't too much clutter. From where she stood in the living room, she saw a hallway to the right—where Jack had disappeared about thirty seconds ago—and the opening to the kitchen to her left.

Jack came back into the room, looking a little embarrassed. "Sorry about that," he said. "Now, what do you need to know about Nick Sanders?"

"Well, he's the prime suspect in a case my partner and I are working on. We're finding out some things about him from just about everywhere. And before we have a solid case against him, we need to find out every detail about his time here in Duck Branch."

"Well, he came in as a worker for Bill a few years ago from what I heard. I was in between jobs earlier last year and Bill took me on. The job sort of stuck and I ended up staying there for a pretty good amount of time. But the whole time I was there, Nick just got on my damned nerves. He's just that's kind of guy. Really unlikable, you know?"

"Anything in particular?"

"Well, he was a hard worker, I'll give him that. But he also had this holier than thou thing going…which made no sense to me because he was clearly always high or drunk or something. I will say this, though…there was one day where he just randomly opened up to me about his wife dying. A heroin overdose, he said."

"Did he ever mention any other family members?" Kate asked.

"You know, he did. And I just thought it was him trying to make up this other life. Sort of trying to make us think he was important. He told us about some daughter he had that had gotten away. He said she'd gone missing or something. Talked about how he was going to get her back, make up with his *other* daughter, too, and start a new life. He'd get emotional over it, but not in the way a normal person would. He'd get violent. Kicking tires, punching cars, things like that. Honestly, he's just a scary dude."

"And you felt he was just making it all up?"

"I did."

"Mr. Kramer, can you tell me what the fight was about a few months back?"

It was the first time Kramer came off as uneasy. He looked to the floor for a moment, a trick Kate had seen multiple times from people who were simply trying to buy time. It wasn't a hard equation; she knew that Nick had been doing hard drugs and selling them as well. It wasn't a stretch to assume that Jack Kramer might have been one of his customers.

"I assure you, I am only here to find out information about Mr. Sanders. Anything you may have been involved with concerning him will not be held against you."

Jack eyed her skeptically and let out a sigh. "I loaned him some money. Well, I didn't *loan* it to him…I gave him some to score me some pot. He said he could get the really good stuff, you know?"

Kate was fairly certain that Nick Sanders didn't waste his time with pot, but she let it slide. "Did he cheat you?"

"Yeah. He basically stole the money from me and didn't do much to even deny it. Things got heated when I confronted him and we started throwing punches."

"Is that why you quit working for Bill?" Kate asked.

"Partly. I had been talking to the people at my new place of employment for quite a while. The pay is about the same and I have to drive a bit farther but at least I wouldn't have to put up with Nick."

"When he mentioned his family, do you know what he meant when he said he had a daughter that had *gotten away*?"

"No. But I figured if he was telling the truth at all—which I honestly still doubt—he meant she had gotten lost in the foster system or something. I can't quite imagine Nick Sanders being a father."

"Any other altercations between the two of you?"

"No. That was it. I mean we'd argue over work stuff but that was about it. When he wasn't being all pissy and violent, he kept to himself. A moody sort of guy. Just…I don't know. He's not the kind of guy you'd want to hang around with, you know?"

Kate nodded. She did know. She was beginning to get a very good picture into who Nick Sanders was and the more she learned, the more she started to wonder if he had indeed killed Wendy and Alvin Fuller in order to get his daughter back.

"I'll let you finish getting ready for work, Mr. Kramer," she said. "Thank you for your time."

Jack rushed to the door, doing his best to show courtesy by opening the door for her. Kate smiled and made her exit, walking back down the rickety old porch steps. Her mind was already in Richmond, ready to put Nick Sanders away and return to her normal life as soon as she could.

She got into her car and put the keys into the ignition. Before she could turn them, though, something started to churn in her heart. And with it, an inner voice that she had heard before, blaring almost like an alarm.

Wait. Hold on...

She dropped her hand away from the keys and looked to the house. Had she missed something? Her instincts certainly felt that she had. But Jack Kramer checked out. There was no reason for her to investigate him further. If anything, he had given her more nails to slam into Nick Sanders' coffin.

Kate shook the feeling off and started the car. The engine revved and although her mind still reeled toward Richmond she could not help but feel something here had been forgotten.

CHAPTER TWENTY NINE

Mercy could hear footsteps walking outside, and then the sound of a car door opening and closing. She was pretty sure there was a woman driving it. Moments ago, she'd thought she'd heard a woman's voice, very faint as she spoke to her captor.

No, Mercy thought. *Please. Help.*

She tried to actually give voice to these thoughts but the tape was too tight over her mouth.

Don't start the car, Mercy thought. *Don't leave, don't go...*

But then Mercy heard the engine start. She closed her eyes and screamed against the tape. The muted sound rattled in her head until it ached, until it felt like her head would split right in two from the force of it.

Mercy tried to make sense of what was going on. Her captor must have some sort of plan for her, a plan that he kept changing. Last night, he had let her inside and gave her dinner. Cornbread, tomato soup, bacon, and a Coke. She'd eaten so much that she'd nearly gotten sick. He'd invited her to sleep in his house, in his bed, assuring her that he would not rape her. When she had asked instead to sleep on the couch, he'd lost his mind. He'd slapped her hard enough to bust her lip all over again and then ended up giving her his bed while he slept on the couch. He had tied her legs together so she could not escape and had kept his rifle by the couch just in case she managed to walk through the house with any ideas of escape.

But then this morning, he hadn't said a word to her. He had allowed her to eat a bowl of Cheerios and then hauled her out to the barn. There, he'd duct-taped her mouth and then taped her wrists together. He did it all in a hurry and she had prayed the entire time that he'd make a mistake. But no...he had been thorough. Her legs were tied together with just a little slack and her wrists were bound in front of her—the one thing she thought he might have screwed up on because with her bound arms in front of her, she was at least a bit more mobile than she would have been if he had taped them behind her back.

He had been working with the lock on the old trailer at the back of the barn when he heard the car turn onto his driveway. That's when he'd thrown her to the ground, apparently not feeling that he had time to mess with the busted old lock on the trailer. He'd gone to the side of the barn, bent down, and opened up what looked like a trapdoor. He had grabbed her up and nearly thrown her down the shallow set of stairs. She'd hit the ground hard enough to knock the wind out of her. She'd also twisted her right wrist in the fall and it currently ached like hell. Before slamming the hidden door shut, he had looked down at her and said the first words of the morning to her.

"You try coming out and doing anything stupid, I'll rape you and then kill you. Slow. You'll beg for the rifle."

She had believed him but had still tried waddling to the trapdoor. There was a catch on it, but it was bent and warped. She was pretty sure she could just push it open. But then what? Her legs and arms were still tied up. As she studied it and tried to come up with a plan, she could hear the engine of the car. It was fading away as it pulled away, back out toward the road.

Mercy collapsed backward, her legs giving out. For a moment, she was afraid a rush of Cheerios and milk were going to come up out of her stomach, blocked by the tape and ultimately gagging her. But she managed to keep it all down. She focused on her breathing and stared up at the cracks in the floor overhead. Dirty little rays of light spilled in, illuminating the dirt floor of what she assumed had once been a cellar of some kind.

I'm going to die here, she thought. *Maybe not today and maybe not tomorrow, but I don't think he's going to let me go. Maybe at one point he had planned on it...but I think something has changed. I'm going to die here. The only question is if it will be a slow or a quick death.*

Staring up at those boards, Mercy Fuller started to cry for the comfort of a mother she knew was no longer alive. Through the tears, she could no longer hear the car outside, moving further toward the road, the driver oblivious to the young girl trapped in the barn just seventy-five yards to her right.

CHAPTER THIRTY

Kate hit the brake pedal hard enough to jolt her. Through the course of her long career, she had only felt an instinctual tug like this twice before. It was almost like a strange surge of déjà vu, a knowledge that there was something here that she should be recognizing. It was a feeling of something being incomplete...of something important just out of her reach.

The back end of her car was less than two feet from the back road that would take her back to the main highway through Duck Branch. She looked back toward Jack Kramer's house, wondering why she felt so drawn to it.

"Because you missed something," she said out loud. "But what?"

Her heart felt like it was beating straight up into her throat as she put the car back into Drive and crept back up Jack's driveway. This time, she did not focus on the driveway itself or the house sitting at the end of it. She kept her eyes on the edges of the yard, in the tree line and in the tall grass around the edges of the property.

And just like that, she saw what she had missed.

Just off to the right side of the house, partially hidden by tall grass and a bit of deadfall and woodland debris, was an old barn. It looked like a horse barn, complete with the second story up in the rafters. A black hole of an ancient window looked out onto the yard. The barn itself did not look all that ominous. After all, this was the South; hundreds of old structures like this sat all across fields and wooded lots.

But sitting right there, like a ghost on the property of a man who had thrown punches with Nick Sanders, made it a bit more relevant. It wasn't that Kate had not physically seen it upon arriving; she had simply let it blur into the surroundings because she had been so hyper-focused on returning to Richmond to wrap this case and get back to Melissa.

She stopped her car along the side of the driveway. It was still in view of Jack Kramer's house, but he'd really have to make an effort to look for it through his front windows. Before getting out of the car, she texted DeMarco, just in case she was about to make a mistake. She sent the text and then got out of the car. She stayed along the edge of the driveway until she came to the yard. There, she clung to the tree line, hunkering down in the tall grass as she moved toward the barn.

As she reached it, she saw old pieces of lumber scattered in the weeds. There were also old tractor parts and rusted tools strewn about. She looked back to the house, saw that there was no sign of Jack, and tried the barn door. Given the age of the barn and the condition of most of the boards that comprised its structure, Kate was not all that surprised to find that the door opened easily. It creaked a bit on its hinges but opened up without a problem.

She stepped inside and within two seconds of looking around, felt that her instincts had led her down the right path once again.

There was an old storage trailer at the back of the barn, the kind that was often pulled behind trucks when people were moving but did not need an entire U-Haul. The rest of the barn looked practically boring in comparison.

The trailer's door was the rolling kind, similar to a garage door. It was held in place along the back end, just below a small step and what looked to have once served as a bumper. The lock itself was an old Masterlock, battered and scratched up. It was also unlocked, the U-shaped clasp placed into the latch at the bottom of the door, but opened.

Kate removed the lock as quietly as she could, sliding it up out of the latch and setting it on the bumper. She placed her fingers inside the small groove that served as the handle and pushed up. The door slid up easily enough but it squeaked along its track. It wasn't too loud, but loud enough to cause Kate concern. Jack would not hear it from inside, but if he happened to be out in his yard, there was a chance it would have reached his ears.

She didn't bother opening the door all the way, not wanting to make any more noise if she didn't have to. She peered inside and again saw that her instincts were spot on.

In the back of the trailer, she saw several empty wrappers. They were clear and plastic, with an orange design. From the back of the trailer, Kate could see enough to know that they were the wrappers to snack crackers. A few empty water bottles were back there as well. As stealthily as she could, Kate crawled into the trailer and investigated the trash. Unlike the trailer and the lock, the wrapper and the bottles were not old. In fact, there were still a few drops of water sitting in the bottom of one of the bottles.

These had not been in here for any longer than a few days. The still-orange cracker crumbs in the trailer floor were further proof of this.

Kate turned and stepped out of the trailer. It was far too easy to imagine Mercy Fuller in there, eating those crackers and drinking that water. But nothing seemed to line up. Why would a man who worked with Nick Sanders have any reason to abduct his daughter?

You can get those answers later, she thought. *For now, get what answers you can from the creep that lives here.*

Kate took quick and quiet steps to the bran door, drawing her Glock. It was eerie how easily the motion came back to her—and how comfortable she felt with it in her hands. She slipped out of the barn door and stayed low, crouched in the tall grass. She inched her way along until she was square with the backyard. A screen door sat along the back, above a set of old wooden stairs.

She had no way of telling where Nick was inside of the house, so she was just going to have to make a run for it. If he saw her, it wouldn't be too big of a deal. After all, she was armed.

And if he's been hiding a fifteen-year-old girl in his barn, he probably is, too, she thought.

She came to the back door and opened the screen. Another door sat behind it, closed. She tried the knob and found it unlocked. She moved quietly, grimacing as she turned the knob all the way. She pushed the door lightly open, just a crack. Concentrating, she could hear Jack Kramer moving around inside. It sounded like he was closer to the front of the house.

With catlike speed that surprised her, Kate slipped through the back door. Her hands gripped the Glock as her heart hammered in her chest. She found herself standing in the kitchen. She could see the living room ahead of her, through the entryway of the kitchen. She could see—

Something came rushing at her from the left, just off of the hallway Jack had gone down to put on a shirt. She raised her Glock but was about a split second too slow. Something crashed into her head. Something hard, something that made a sick thudding noise against her skull.

The pain lasted only a moment. She felt herself slipping away and tried to fight against it. She saw a blurred representation of Jack Kramer's face as she tried to stay on her feet but his features slid away like mud into the darkness that quickly leapt up to claim her.

CHAPTER THIRTY ONE

Something was stinging her face. Stinging or burning or…she wasn't sure.

It was faint at first but then it felt like something exploding. Her face went hard to the right. The sound that accompanied the stinging made Kate aware that she was being slapped. This knowledge caused her eyes to snap wide open. She saw that she was in the barn, sitting in an old wooden chair. She tried to stand but found that she was tied to it. She rocked a bit, nearly toppling the chair, before she was slapped again.

She cried out against it and realized that she made very little sound. Her mouth was taped up, her lips drawn tight together. This brought everything snapping into place, helping her to finally get all of her senses about her. Jack Kramer was standing in front of her. There was a maniacal smile on his face as he hunched down slightly to look in her eyes. Behind him, propped against the edge of the barn door, was a hunting rifle.

"You sure are a nosy bitch, aren't you?" he asked with a smile. "You got the information you needed and left. What the hell did you come back for?"

He raised his hand and she thought he was going to slap her again. Instead, he stepped forward and cupped her by the back of the head. He leaned in closer, their noses less than three inches apart.

"If it makes you feel any better, you did find her," he said. "She's here. Right under our feet if you can believe it." With that comment, he stomped on the floor. The creaky boards beneath them rattled a bit and a plume of dust kicked up. Behind it all, Kate thought she *could* hear some sort of muffled complaint—perhaps from a feminine voice that was also taped shut.

"I'm glad you came, Kate. I really am."

He stepped back away from her again and showed her the ID and badge he had apparently taken from her while she had been knocked out. He tossed them on the floor at her feet where they slid against the wood. He then reached behind him and pulled her Glock out from the waist of his pants.

"This," he said, "I'm keeping. I might just put a bullet between little Mercy's eyes. I wonder what sort of things might happen to you if a bullet from your gun is found in her head. I thought about doing it this morning with my old rifle," he said, nodding to the rifle Kate had seen propped against the edge of the barn door behind him. "Then it would be all over. I could be done with this fucking mess I somehow ended up in."

He seemed to think about this for a moment before he reached into his pocket and pulled out the lock-pick she carried in her inner pocket. "This seems a little old-school, I think," he added.

He tossed the pick to the floor, where it bounced somewhere out of sight. He then hunkered down in front of her and placed his hands on her knees. He caressed her there, rough enough to let her know that she was likely in some very big trouble.

"I'm very glad you came," he said again. "I never really knew what I was going to do with Mercy once I had her here. I certainly wasn't going to just hand her over to her stupid father, now was I? That girl is somewhere way beyond sexy but...you know, I'm a man of high moral standing. I've been fighting it...I have...but I just can't do anything like that to her. But you...shit, I think you're probably older than I am. Fifty? Fifty-five, maybe? And there's a whole lot of things I want to do to Mercy that I think I could manage to do to you just fine."

A million things went pouring through Kate's mind in that moment. First, she wondered how long she had been knocked out and what he had hit her with. Her head didn't hurt too badly at the moment, but given the vicious slaps he had given her, that did not surprise her. She then wondered how long it would be before DeMarco got worried and came out to help. And lastly, she wondered if Mercy Fuller was indeed in this barn, right under her feet as Jack had suggested.

He suddenly reached out and cupped her face in his hand. He leaned in again and Kate was certain he was going to kiss her. "I can call in sick," he said. "I'm already late...so I can call in sick and you and I can have some fun together. And maybe when I'm done, you can tell me what I need to do with Mercy to make sure the FBI doesn't come looking for me. Because make no mistake about it: if you have any hope of leaving this place alive, you sure as hell aren't going to let anyone know what you found out here...who I've been keeping." He smiled at her again, revealing teeth that indicated he, too, had been enjoying some of the same drugs as Nick Sanders. "Do you believe me, Kate?"

She nodded, but only because she knew it was her only chance. If she was going to get out of this, she had to make him think he was in control.

149

Not just for her sake, but for Mercy Fuller's as well.

***

Mercy had sat as still as a stone when the man had brought the lady into the barn. She had to sit. The cellar was more like a crawlspace. It wasn't even tall enough for her to stand up in…which made it very hard to move around on her tied legs. She figured there might be four and a half feet between the floor and the ceiling—probably closer to four.

The man had been speaking to the woman angrily, but would chuckle every now and then. He had even spoken to Mercy, too, letting her know they had some company. Mercy had no idea who the woman was or why she was here…not until he had started ranting, letting the woman—Kate, apparently—know what he planned to do to her. He mentioned the FBI and how she had better stay quiet.

She's with the FBI, Mercy thought. *My God, I might get out of here after all.*

It was a faint glimmer of hope. After all, the agent was now tied to a chair, silenced with the same tape that was around her face, and being slapped around. It was a desperate situation and it dawned on her that there were now two of them. They could maybe work together and…

Mercy looked to her right where something had fallen through the cracks of the floor a few moments ago. The man had been showing Kate that he had her badge and ID, her gun, and something else he had called old-school. Whatever that had been, it had bounced on the floor almost musically over her head before rolling through a crack in the floor and striking the dirt floor.

She'd thought nothing of it at first but was now thinking that if her abductor had taken it off of the agent, it might be useful. Mercy walked over to it, shuffling her legs in what she was sure must be a very comical way since they were still tied together and she could not stand up completely. She craned her neck to see where the woman was in position to the thing that had fallen. Mercy could see slight movement through the boards just a few feet overhead and to her left. She then looked away and to the floor. It was much darker down here than it had been on the barn's main floor but she could make out the basic shape of it.

She wasn't sure what it was at first, not until she got down on her knees. She was able to reach down and pick it up, again thankful that her captor had taped her wrists together in front of her rather than behind. She clumsily turned the object around in her fingers, unsure of what it was. It was long and slightly cylindrical, just a little longer than a key. The head of it was almost shaped like a key and that was the clue that told her what she was holding in her hands. It was some sort of tool to help pick locks.

She felt defeated. The tool was absolutely useless to her. It wasn't like she was tied together with locks, now was it?

But after that initial defeat passed, she realized that if she could angle her fingers right and maybe bend her wrists awkwardly, she might be able to puncture the loop of duct tape that had been placed around her wrists.

It took her a few moments to bend her fingers just right. She dropped the pick several times in trying to find the right position. When she had it, she shuffle-stepped over to the wall. It was mostly dirt just like the floor but with wooden struts running up the side here and there. She braced her back against one of these struts to take the burden of standing on her tied-together legs and started trying to push the head of the pick through the tape.

Above her, the man slapped Kate again. The sound surprised Mercy, causing her to drop the pick once more. With tears brimming in her eyes, she bent down to pick it up.

You can do this, you can do this. Just concentrate…

She took a deep shaky breath and started again. She pushed until her fingers ached but it did not seem to be working.

But then she felt a slight bit of give. She pulled the pick back carefully, pinched between the knuckled of her pointer and middle fingers and then lowly pushed it forward again.

She heard the slight *pop* as the pick push through the tape. She carefully continued to push until she felt the pick brush against the skin of her inner wrist.

She started to saw with the pick, working her way upward. She knew that if she sawed at least half of it, she'd be able to tear free. But it was slow work and the more she tried at it, the more she sweat. And the more she sweat, the harder it was to saw. But she had to…she had no choice. And as she did, she listened as her captor rambled on over her head.

Each word was like a dagger as he started to talk about her parents but even then, she focused on sawing through the tape with the little pick. Even when she could barely see through the tears that started to spill, she sawed and sawed with her sweaty, trembling fingers.

***

151

The thing that scared Kate the most was that she did not think Jack Kramer was crazy. Not in any real definable way. He apparently had issues with women, as evidenced by his holding two captive and currently beating the hell out of one who just happened to be fifty-six years old. But *crazy*...she wasn't so sure.

"It seemed like a good idea at the time," Jack said. "That idiot told me about this estranged daughter of his but there was another one...a daughter that he told me just sort of slipped away. But one night over beers, I got it out of him. Someone had stolen her from him, some family in a shithole called Deton. He said he wanted to get her back but I knew he never would. That would be responsibility...that would be catering to someone's needs other than his own. But I started to think...what if I used the story as blackmail? What if I found the couple that took her and asked for some money? They pay up or I'd go to the news."

He smiled, perhaps at what he thought of as the genius of the plan. He started to pace, walking over to an old work bench along the side of the barn. He picked up something from it, something that looked like an old hammer. He hefted it in his hand and came back to her. He showed her the hammer as if he were offering it to her as a gift.

And then he brought it down hard just above her bent knee. The pain was immense, and she was thankful that it only hit meat. It wasn't a vicious blow, not one that he was using to seriously hurt her, but a rover of static-like shocks went blasting through her leg.

"You're tough," he said. "That's good. You and I...we're going to have a lot of fun."

He licked his lips, using the hammer to trace a line from the bottom of her throat to just beneath her breasts.

"I didn't want to kill them," he said. "I thought they were actually going to give me the money. Started to talk real serious about it. But then the husband got all mouthy and scared. We got into a fight and I killed him. Shot him right in the throat and then in the head. Only had one bullet left for the wife. I put it in her belly and then clubbed her to death with the butt of the gun."

He looked almost remorseful here. But after a moment of what Kate thought might be his form of self-reflection, he shrugged. "I had to get rough with Mercy. Punched her in the stomach then punched her in the face. She went out like a light. After that, it was easy. Walked right through the backyard with her over my shoulder and straight to my truck. I parked a pretty good distance away, on

152

some dirt road in the middle of nowhere. Hell…a town like that, no one saw me come or go. I came in and left like a fucking ghost."

The exposition was almost gratuitous. But Kate had seen this before. He was trying to talk himself up. He was trying to convince himself that he was smart…that his smarts back in Deton (as well as his savagery, perhaps) had gotten him out of there without leaving a trace. If he could relive that high, he would probably convince himself that raping and killing and FBI agent was well within his wheelhouse, too.

"So now the question is what to do with little Mercy. Do I just keep her? I don't want to kill her. Truth be told, killing her parents wasn't what I thought it would be. I'd only killed once before…an old homeless drunk that tried to mug me. I don't enjoy it. But I had to. If I had have just left the Fullers' house that night and—"

He was cut short by a sudden pounding noise. The entire floor felt as if it was shaking. For a brief moment, Kate wondered if the shoddy floor was actually collapsing.

"What the hell?" Jack said.

He looked to the right. Kate's eyes followed his gaze and she saw the slight rise in the floor, as well as the old rusty hinge that was mostly embedded in the floor.

A trapdoor, Kate thought. *Or an old cellar door or something like that. Mercy might indeed be down there.*

As if in response, the floor seemed to quake again. Kate saw that it was because something was hammering against that door. It jumped up, banging the latch and the hinge that kept it closed. Kate figured if something struck it hard enough from the other side, the whole thing would just splinter away from the hinge and the floor.

It's Mercy, Kate thought. *But what the hell is she doing?*

Jack let out a small roar as he stormed over to the door. As he neared it, he reached to his back, for the Glock. He leaned down, taking a key out of his pocket, and unfastened the lock—which, Kate saw, was just as old and battered as the one she had seen on the back of the trailer that sat behind her.

Kate could see what was going to happen. He was going to open that door and shoot her with a bureau-issued firearm. This was going to end terribly.

And she was also very aware that she may not live to see how it all played out.

***

153

Mercy was hunched down, waiting. The tape from her wrists and mouth were in a pile on the dirt floor to her right, beside the ropes she had untied from her legs. She was free, waiting like a coiled snake for that motherfucker to open the trapdoor. She held the lock pick in her right hand, holding it like a very small knife. It felt like a pathetic little weapon but she figured it she struck hard enough, the size would not matter at all.

She heard his footfalls coming towards the door, thundering toward her. Specks of dust and debris fell between the floorboards, raining down on her. He was muttering curses under his breath as he approached. As he drew closer, the trapdoor over her head shuddered in its weak mildewed frame.

She listened as he knelt down and rattled the latch. There was a click as it was freed and then the square of the door was washed in murky light. Mercy felt the muscles in her legs tightening, ready to pounce, ready to do whatever was necessary to get out of here.

Slowly, his face came into view as he peered down.

Mercy wasted no time. She sprang up fast and hard, bringing the lock-pick with her. Her eyes were closed but she felt the pick slam into his face. His scream was what forced her to open her eyes. When she did, she saw him teetering on the edge of the frame. The pick had taken him just below the eye and her hand still held the handle. With a final scream, Mercy shoved forward even harder. She felt bone give away and something soft starting to also yield behind that.

He tried to retreat, but Mercy had one last burst of bravery. As he was floundering around, trying to make sense of what happened, Mercy grabbed his left arm, still propping up his weight on the edge of the trapdoor frame, and pulled.

He came crashing down through the doorway. His left leg struck her shoulder but she barely noticed. He was still screaming, his hands going to his face where the lock-pick was still sticking out.

Mercy wasted no time in watching him. She reached up and grabbed the frame of the trapdoor. She planted both hands on each side and pulled herself up. She did it with such frantic energy and nerves that she nearly catapulted herself out of the cellar. She came out with such force that she toppled over, her legs striking the entryway to the cellar. She wheeled back around and slammed the trapdoor shut. She saw the lock and slammed the U-bolt home, trapping him down there.

Directly in front of her, about ten feet away, was the FBI agent. She was bound to a chair with rope and her arms were tied together with the same duct tape that had been around her own wrist only a few moments ago.

She moved so quickly to the agent that she stumbled and almost fell. Her captor's screams continued to belt out from the trapdoor, cursing and wailing, screams of horrendous pain and bloodcurdling hatred.

The agent—*Kate,* Mercy remembered again from having heard her captor say it—was shaking her head as Mercy approached her. Kate nodded quickly to the door, trying to get Mercy to escape. And God help her, Mercy nearly did. But she could not leave this poor woman here—this woman who had come to save her. There was no way Mercy could leave her behind.

She approached the chair and looked at the ropes. They were tied tightly around the back of the chair, pulling Kate tightly against it. But the knots were fairly obvious. She worked quickly, a little surprised at how simple the knots were. Apparently, he had been far too interested in what he could do to his new prisoner than applying tighter, more effective knots.

The first loops came away and then the second. But the third was harder. It was then that Kate made a mewling noise through the tape around her mouth. She then held up her arms, showing Mercy the tape. She nodded to the tape and Mercy instantly forgot the ropes and started tearing at the tape. Her hands were sweaty, making it hard to attack it, but she was still fueled on adrenaline and nerves, so tearing it was rather easy. She almost had it, focusing on the tape rather than the terrified look in Kate's eyes.

A gunshot sounded out from below them. The a second. Behind the echo of the second shot, Mercy heard a clattering noise. She looked over toward the trapdoor and saw the two holes in the floor—one of which had torn the hinge and lock directly away from the trapdoor.

The door then swung open. One hand came up and then the other. And then he was there, his face leering out over the edge of the frame and looking at her.

Mercy froze, her heart feeling as if it had stopped beating. She tried to will her hands to move but there was nothing. She was absolutely frozen as he pulled himself up out of the cellar with Kate's gun in his right hand.

CHAPTER THIRTY TWO

Kate had no idea what had gone on between Mercy and Jack when he had gone to the trapdoor, but it was clear that Mercy had gotten the upper hand. She had rarely heard screams of pain like the ones that came barreling up out of the cellar as Mercy had worked at the ropes around the chair.

She wanted to tell the girl to run, to save herself, but the tape was blocking her mouth. She wished the girl would have taken that off first but did not fault her for doing her best. Given the situation, Mercy was operating miraculously.

But then the gunshots tore through the barn and Mercy had frozen. She'd nearly removed the tape from Kate's wrists as the trapdoor came flying open and Jack Kramer's hands appeared at the edges.

Recognizing the shock that had seized Mercy, Kate knew she had to run things now. The tape around her wrists was ripped a little more than halfway down. It looked as if Jack had wrapped it three layers deep, making it quite hard for Kate to pull it apart on her own. She summoned all of her strength and started to pull as hard as she could. There was much more give than before but it would still not tear free.

She looked back to Mercy and saw that the girl was literally frozen in place. She was in shock and, if things went that way, she'd likely stand in that same position until Jack came up out of the cellar and started firing on them.

Across the room, she could now see Jack's face as he pulled himself out of the hole. She saw the gruesome wound where Mercy had apparently stabbed him with something just below the left eye. And she also saw her Glock in his right hand as he pulled himself shakily back up to the floor.

Kate continued to pull at the tape, trying to get it to stretch and rip even further. She channeled all of the strength from her shoulders and her core, crying out behind the tape. She pulled until she felt the muscles in her forearms cramping, until she thought her wrist might snap.

But then the tape ripped. And then it ripped some more. The sound it made was heavenly and seemed to send one last surge of strength through Kate's forearms. With one final pull, the tape tore in half in the front. One final pull tore the back of it away from her right wrist, leaving it in a clump that dangled from her left wrist.

She fell forward right away, her knees striking the floor as the chair was still attached to her back by that last loop of rope. Still, she slammed into Mercy, shoving her into action. The girl snapped out of it just as Jack pulled himself through the doorway. He was up to his chest now, struggling to get his lower half up through the door.

With her hands free, Kate easily slipped out of the last loop of rope around the chair. When her back was free of it, she did the only thing that she could think of…the first thing that came to mind. It seemed silly at the time but proved to be effective.

She grabbed the chair and threw it as hard as she could in the direction of the trapdoor. It bounced, breaking the right armrest, right before it hit the opening. Although it did not strike Jack, it caused him to instinctively release the sides of the trapdoor frame to protect himself. When he did, he fell back against it and started to fall back into the darkness.

He fought for balance and though he managed to keep from falling back into the cellar, it gave Kate just enough time.

She dove for the barn door, directly for the rifle Jack and propped up there—the one she had sensed right away when he had slapped her back into consciousness. Even before she grabbed it, she managed to study it for all of a second, making sure she knew how to use it when she held it. It was an old hunting rifle and the hammer at the back was disengaged. She took it up, steadied herself against the barn wall, and cocked the hammer back.

Jack saw this and raised his right arm. For a moment, Kate saw her own service weapon pointed at her. But Jack had not properly regained his balance yet and could not focus his aim.

Kate fired. The blast was impossibly loud and the jolt of the recoil was stronger than she had expected. But Kate's aim had been true. The shot took Jack in the center of his chest. He bucked backward and slumped down, falling back into the cellar. The sound of his body hitting the first was drowned out by the ringing in her ears caused by the rifle blast.

Kate dropped the rifle and brought her hands to her mouth. She tore the tape away as she did her best to take stock of Mercy Fuller. The girl had done her best to escape the barn. But something—probably he rifle blast—had caused her to freeze up again. She was lying half in and half out of the shed, her trembling body lying on the ground just beside the partially open door.

"It's okay," she told Mercy. And while she knew this to be true, Kate found that she was having trouble getting to her feet. The surge of adrenaline and emotion was just too much for her muscles and nerves to comprehend.

So Kate just reached over and placed a hand on the girl's shoulder. "Mercy…it's okay. He's gone. Are you all right?"

Mercy responded by letting out a piercing wail. She curled herself into a little ball and started to sob uncontrollably. They were wails of loss and grief and terror, all coming out at once.

Not knowing what else to do, Kate pulled herself closer to Mercy and placed an arm around her, holding her closely to her. She thought of her phone, sitting in the car. She needed to call DeMarco, but she figured that could wait a few more minutes. She kept her eyes on the trapdoor, pretty certain Jack Kramer would not be making another appearance but wanting to be sure all the same. She sat there just outside of the old barn, in the tall grass, holding Mercy close.

She figured it was the least she could do. The girl had probably saved her life. And because Mercy would have no mother to receive this sort of consoling from when this was all wrapped up, Kate was more than happy to provide it in the meantime.

CHAPTER THIRTY THREE

Kate was sitting in the back of an ambulance, her legs dangling out over the bumper, when Sheriff Barnes came over. She had just finished enduring a check-up with one of the paramedics to ensure she had no internal injuries or concussions. Other than some bruising on her face from the barrage of slaps from Jack Kramer, she was doing just fine.

"A little outside of your jurisdiction, aren't you?" she asked him.

"I headed out as soon as your partner called to fill me in. Sadly, this little place is far too much like Deton. I felt I had to come, though. I wanted to thank you for closing this case. I know it wasn't quite the ending we were hoping for, but at least we have answers now."

"It didn't end too badly," she said, looking over to the edge of Jack Kramer's yard. There was a group of people huddled around Mercy Fuller, who sat on the back of a patrol car. DeMarco was one of the people in that group. She hadn't strayed too far from Mercy's side since she arrived on the scene.

"Yeah, we came out of it with Mercy Fuller still alive," Barnes conceded. "How are *you* doing?"

"A little shaken. I want to get back home, but I feel like I need to see what happens with Mercy."

"That girl is one hell of a fighter," Barnes said. "Did they tell you what she used to stab Kramer with?"

"They did. A lock-pick. *My* lock-pick. It must have fallen through one of the cracks between the floor boards when he was throwing my stuff on the ground."

It looked as if Barnes wanted to say something else. But in the end, he settled for an encouraging soft clap to her back and a smile of appreciation. He then walked over to where the small group was stull huddled around Mercy.

Kate looked in that direction as she hopped down out of the ambulance. Mercy was looking over the heads of the six different people standing around her. Her eyes finally found Kate. She offered a forced smile, but never took her eyes off of the agent who had come out here to the middle of nowhere to find her.

It brought tears to Kate's eye, but they were happy tears. As she wiped them away, she caught Mercy smiling at her. This time, it was genuine.

The girl broke away from the little group and started over toward Kate. Those around her started to reach for her, to keep her stationary, until they realized where she was headed. Kate put an arm around her instinctively when the girl reached her.

"The sheriff told me he'd help me with anything regarding social services," Mercy said. "He said it in this kind of pained way, like he was hiding something." She looked down at her feet and, as if embarrassed, added: "I know about my parents. Well, I mean, I know there's some question about if Mom and Dad are my real...my real..."

"How do you know that?"

"A man claiming to be my real dad called a few weeks ago. Left a message. I never called him back."

"What did the message say?"

"That he was my real father and the Fullers were liars and thieves."

"Did you believe him?"

Mercy shrugged, leaning into Kate. "I don't know. I...well, there would be times when I would look at my mom and dad and realize I looked nothing like them. And there aren't any baby pictures of me around the house. I just...something never felt quite right. And it got stronger the older I got."

"So you *did* believe him?"

"No. Not at first. But all of this...what happened...Agent Wise, was he right? Was he telling the truth?"

Kate bit back a sob when she realized she was going to have to be the one to tell her. She took the girl by the hand and then looked over at the small crowd by the car. She gave Barnes a little nod and then looked down at Mercy.

"Let's take a little walk," she said.

Mercy nodded, and the look in her eyes told Kate that she already knew what was coming. But she walked with Kate anyway, up the little driveway. They walked hand-in-hand as Mercy Fuller slowly but surely learned the true history of her life.

***

Kate got the text eight days later. She was huddled up under a blanket on the back porch of a cabin in the Blue Ridge Mountains when it came in. Allen was beside her, an arm draped around her

160

waist. Somewhere below them, a vineyard wound its way through the valleys as the sun started to set behind the peaks around them.

The text was from Barnes, notifying her that Mercy Fuller had been placed in the care of the state of Virginia and had already been placed into a foster home. He also let her know that the family that was taking Mercy in had a track record for treating their foster kids exceptionally well. In fact, they had taken Mercy in because they had just sent their previous foster kid off to college.

She read the message and smiled. She then set the phone down and snuggled up next to Allen. The plan was to watch the sunset out on the back porch and then, if their backs and knees (and the chilly mountain temperature) allowed, to make love under the blankets.

"Good news?" Allen asked, noticing her smile.

"Very good. Mercy found a good home. I think she's going to be okay."

"That's *fantastic* news," he said.

"She's also going to meet with Katherine Sanders…her biological sister."

Kate smiled and looked up at the sun, slowly sinking behind the mountains. An entire spectrum of gold and oranges and light pinks had started to filter through the atmosphere, highlighted along the mountain peaks.

Good news seemed to be trending. Just yesterday, Kate had gone to the doctor with Melissa. Little Michelle had undergone some more tests and had come out absolutely fine. The indicators of the cancer they had feared just two weeks ago were now nowhere to be seen. There would be a follow-up test in six weeks but after that, the scare would be over and they would be out of the woods.

"You know," Allen said, "I know that what happened in that barn did something to you. You're different. Not distant…not really. But there's something. Maybe we need to talk about it before we head back home?"

She knew he was right. She had talked some of it out with DeMarco, but had kept it all at a surface level. Even when she had debriefed with Duran, where she had to go into more detail, she had not delved into the emotional turmoil of it all.

"Yeah, I think we must," she said. "Maybe later tonight, in the hot tub."

"I'm going to hold you to that," he said.

She fully expected him to. And that was why she could so easily kiss him under the setting sun, moving closer into him to start with the final step of that evening's plans. As they began, the sky showed off a whole range of colors as dusk settled in, pulling in the night. By the time they were done, the first of the stars had come out, shining fiercely. Kate looked up at them and something about their unblemished shine in the clear mountain sky reminded her of the slight sparkle she had seen in Mercy Fuller's eyes when they had shared the one final smile.

It was a glimmer she often saw in Michelle's eyes...a little girl who didn't even know what cancer was yet had lived through a cancer scare.

It was as if those first stars of the night were speaking to her, telling her that there was reason to go on—reason to continue working to help others, to keep that glimmer of hope in the eyes of people like Mercy Fuller and all of the others who far too often could not help themselves.

IF SHE FLED
(A Kate Wise Mystery—Book 5)

"A masterpiece of thriller and mystery. Blake Pierce did a magnificent job developing characters with a psychological side so well described that we feel inside their minds, follow their fears and cheer for their success. Full of twists, this book will keep you awake until the turn of the last page."
--Books and Movie Reviews, Roberto Mattos (re Once Gone)

IF SHE FLED (A Kate Wise Mystery) is book #5 in a new psychological thriller series by bestselling author Blake Pierce, whose #1 bestseller Once Gone (Book #1) (a free download) has received over 1,000 five star reviews.

When another 50 year old woman is found dead in her home in a wealthy suburb—the second such victim in just two months— the FBI is stumped. They must turn to their most brilliant mind—retired FBI agent Kate Wise, 55—to come back to the line of duty and solve it.

What do these two empty nesters have in common? Were they targeted?

How long until this serial killer strikes again?

And is Kate, though past her prime, still able to solve cases that no one else can?

An action-packed thriller with heart-pounding suspense, IF SHE FLED is book #5 in a riveting new series that will leave you turning pages late into the night.

Book #6 in the KATE WISE MYSTERY SERIES will be available soon.

Blake Pierce

Blake Pierce is author of the bestselling RILEY PAGE mystery series, which includes fourteen books (and counting). Blake Pierce is also the author of the MACKENZIE WHITE mystery series, comprising eleven books (and counting); of the AVERY BLACK mystery series, comprising six books; of the KERI LOCKE mystery series, comprising five books; of the MAKING OF RILEY PAIGE mystery series, comprising four books (and counting); of the KATE WISE mystery series, comprising five books (and counting); of the CHLOE FINE psychological suspense mystery, comprising four books (and counting); and of the JESSE HUNT psychological suspense thriller series, comprising four books (and counting).

An avid reader and lifelong fan of the mystery and thriller genres, Blake loves to hear from you, so please feel free to visit www.blakepierceauthor.com to learn more and stay in touch.

BOOKS BY BLAKE PIERCE

A JESSIE HUNT PSYCHOLOGICAL SUSPENSE SERIES
THE PERFECT WIFE (Book #1)
THE PERFECT BLOCK (Book #2)
THE PERFECT HOUSE (Book #3)
THE PERFECT SMILE (Book #4)

CHLOE FINE PSYCHOLOGICAL SUSPENSE SERIES
NEXT DOOR (Book #1)
A NEIGHBOR'S LIE (Book #2)
CUL DE SAC (Book #3)
SILENT NEIGHBOR (Book #4)

KATE WISE MYSTERY SERIES
IF SHE KNEW (Book #1)
IF SHE SAW (Book #2)
IF SHE RAN (Book #3)
IF SHE HID (Book #4)
IF SHE FLED (Book #5)

THE MAKING OF RILEY PAIGE SERIES
WATCHING (Book #1)
WAITING (Book #2)
LURING (Book #3)
TAKING (Book #4)

RILEY PAIGE MYSTERY SERIES
ONCE GONE (Book #1)
ONCE TAKEN (Book #2)
ONCE CRAVED (Book #3)
ONCE LURED (Book #4)
ONCE HUNTED (Book #5)
ONCE PINED (Book #6)
ONCE FORSAKEN (Book #7)
ONCE COLD (Book #8)
ONCE STALKED (Book #9)
ONCE LOST (Book #10)
ONCE BURIED (Book #11)
ONCE BOUND (Book #12)
ONCE TRAPPED (Book #13)
ONCE DORMANT (Book #14)

ONCE SHUNNED (Book #15)

MACKENZIE WHITE MYSTERY SERIES
BEFORE HE KILLS (Book #1)
BEFORE HE SEES (Book #2)
BEFORE HE COVETS (Book #3)
BEFORE HE TAKES (Book #4)
BEFORE HE NEEDS (Book #5)
BEFORE HE FEELS (Book #6)
BEFORE HE SINS (Book #7)
BEFORE HE HUNTS (Book #8)
BEFORE HE PREYS (Book #9)
BEFORE HE LONGS (Book #10)
BEFORE HE LAPSES (Book #11)
BEFORE HE ENVIES (Book #12)

AVERY BLACK MYSTERY SERIES
CAUSE TO KILL (Book #1)
CAUSE TO RUN (Book #2)
CAUSE TO HIDE (Book #3)
CAUSE TO FEAR (Book #4)
CAUSE TO SAVE (Book #5)
CAUSE TO DREAD (Book #6)

KERI LOCKE MYSTERY SERIES
A TRACE OF DEATH (Book #1)
A TRACE OF MUDER (Book #2)
A TRACE OF VICE (Book #3)
A TRACE OF CRIME (Book #4)
A TRACE OF HOPE (Book #5)

CPSIA information can be obtained
at www.ICGtesting.com
Printed in the USA
BVHW082311170821
614515BV00009B/699

9 781094 309996